This Diary Belongs to:
Tita de la Garza.
Ciudad Porfirio Díaz,
1910

Tita's Diary

September 2020

The Publishing Portal
Los Angeles, California.
www.thepublishingportal.com

ISBN: 978-1-7347706-7-4 (paperback)
978-1-7347706-8-1 (ebook)

Library of Congress Control Number: 2020915233

Printed in the United States of America

*This is me, standing
next to mother.*

Otomí Hñañu Poem

In the drop of dew does the sun shine:
the drop of dew then dries.
In my eyes, my own, you shine:
and I am alive.

Khasa-tuyhiadimiyottzi:
sa-tuhmotti
Khanöm da goquiyottzi:
Nügo, nügodibui

July fourth, 1910

Dear Diary, forgive me for not using you sooner, but I felt like I had nothing interesting to write. However, something happened today that I feel will change my life forever. I went to the mass celebrating Our Lady Refuge of Sinners, who is of course the patron of our city... and I saw Love! So bright it blinded me. No matter where I looked, a bright circle of light was present, even when my eyelids were shut. Where did I see such love, you ask? In the eyes of Pedro Múzquiz! It was very strange, because Pedro and I have seen each other many times since we were small children, but this time it was special. His gaze was like a fiery lightning bolt that got me so flustered I had to avert my eyes. Later, I was asked to help Father Ignacio gather the tithe. When I approached the bench where

Don Pascual and Pedro were sitting, Pascual gave his son a banknote to give to me, and when Pedro put it in the basket he deliberately brushed my hand with his fingers. My body quivered from head to toe. I've never felt anything similar in my 15 years of existence and something inside me told me that Pedro was destined to be the man of my life.

Dear Diary,

Today there was a party at my house and Don Pascual and Pedro came. Mother asked me to fetch a tray of fritters from the kitchen and Pedro kindly offered to help. He used our time alone as an opportunity to declare his love for me! I was at a loss of words and told him I would think about it. He responded that love is not something you think about, you either feel it or you don't, and he is correct. When he looks at me I can't think of anything other than what I'm feeling, which must be what fritter dough feels like when it comes in contact with boiling oil.
I finally said yes in a hurry, as I heard mother entering the kitchen.

Fritters

Boil a litre of water with the skins of four green tomatoes, taking care to not boil for to long lest it become bitter. This water should then be mixed with one kilogram of flour, one tablespoon baking powder, one egg, half a cup of oil and a pinch of salt. Once the dough is formed it must be pounded against the table several times until it is soft and spongy. Then it must be shaped into a ball and let stand for one hour. Once the dough no longer sticks to your hands, that means it's ready for the next step. Roll several small balls of dough and use a rolling pin to flatten them on a table that has been previously sprinkled with flour. When the dough is thin enough it should be further stretched over one's knee or in the bottom of a clay pot with the help of a wet cloth. In the meantime, heat oil in a pot.

Once the oil is boiling, introduce the fritters until they are golden-brown. When they are removed from the oil they must be sprinkled with sugar, and finally bathed in the traditional syrup made with brown sugar, cinnamon, orange zest and a splash of anise liqueur.

Today I confided in my sister Gertrudis about the love that Pedro and I share. She hugged me and we started spinning around as we held hands, until mother saw us and yelled from the balcony: "Girls! Stop spinning, your calves are showing!". It wasn't until that moment that I noticed how my skirt rose with the spinning, and I felt bad.
But as soon as mother went back into the house, Gertrudis raised her skirt up to her hips and shook her bottom from side to side. I had to cover my mouth to stifle my laughter.

Sample for my trousseau

Today I began to work on my trousseau. When my nanny Nacha saw me practice my knitting she made a worried face and lovingly told me to wait until mother authorized my wedding to Pedro before I began knitting anything, and I explained that I prefer to knit and embroider without feeling rushed.
In fact, today I shall buy the yarn to knit my bridal bedspread. I am planning to work on it for a year, which is the amount of time Pedro and I think prudent to plan the wedding.
In the meantime I shall also collect my favorite recipes.

This is what my bedding will look like.

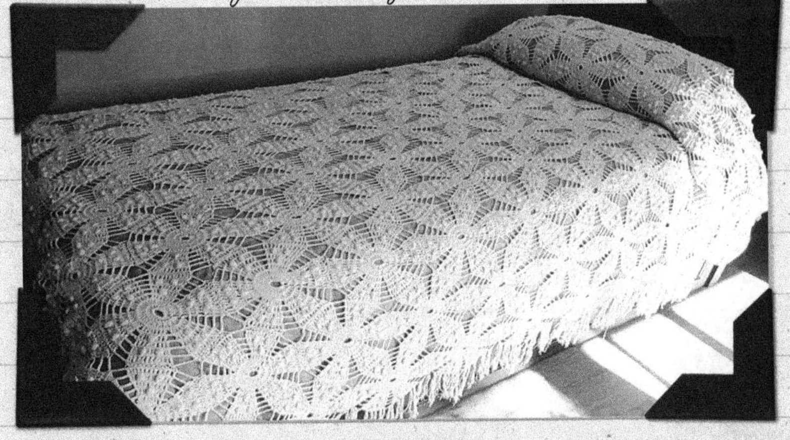

Guess what? Tomorrow is my birthday and we will make Christmas Rolls, but that's not important. What I'm most excited about is that Pedro and his father will ask mother for my hand in marriage. I'm a bit scared. We'll see how it goes. In the meantime, today I designed the seal for our wedding invitations. I like the idea of sealing an envelope with fire. In the time I've spent in the kitchen, I have learned that heat and fire have a transforming effect on matter. Food changes its behavior completely when cooled or heated.

For example, if you add a pinch of sugar to beef while it cooks, it will not only improve its flavor but will also augment the temperature and seal the meat's juices inside. But how is my heart supposed keep my blood from boiling and exploding within me every time Pedro kisses me? That is why I intend to lick every envelope before I close it. I want my saliva to be burnt water. I want the fire of the seal to fan the flames of love in our intertwined initials.

Christmas Rolls

1 can of sardines in tomato paste.
½ kg of chorizo
1 onion
Oregano
1 can of Serrano Chiles
10 rolls

Finely chop onions and serrano chiles. Skin and debone the sardines, taking care to keep them as whole as possible. Fry the chorizo over low heat. When done, remove from fire and add the onions, chiles, and sardines, and let this mixture stand before filling the rolls. It's ideal to let the rolls stand while wrapped in cloth overnight, so the bread will become impregnated with the fat from the chorizo. The next day, before serving, put in the oven for 10 minutes.

Today Pedro and I swore our eternal love to Our Lady Refuge of Sinners. Then we lit a candle and placed it on her altar along with a bouquet of flowers. This was our intimate secret ceremony. Everything went well until we noticed that the gossipy Paquita Lobo was watching us. I hope that she doesn't tell mother.

I'm not allowed to marry because I have to care for mother until she dies?

Where did this tradition come from? Why did no one tell me of it before I fell in love with Pedro?

~~Lo veíamos como [illegible]~~

<u>It's madness!</u>

I have to wait until mother dies so I can love? Why me and not Rosaura? Why should anyone make this sacrifice? Did whoever came up with this idea ever realize that if I don't marry and have children, no one will look after me in my old age? What is the purpose of this? To ensure care for one person while denying another happiness? After all, one cares for others out of love, not out of obligation. How can one love what one hates? And how can one hate what is loved? I really want to hate Pedro. How could he accept to marry Rosaura instead of me? Why? The only thing that's clear to me is that tonight, a moonless night, cold and darkness have settled in my heart.

Today Nacha forbade me from stepping on a corn kernel. She said it was a form of disrespect to the god of corn. I like how she believes that seeds contain invisible gods that benevolently care for nature, but that doesn't quite solve the many doubts I have had inside my head since I was a small girl. I know for a fact that nature harbors intelligence. Seeds know which plant will erupt from within them without anyone having to tell them. Birds know when to fly. Animals know when to mate and how to care for their offspring. It's nice to think that it's the gods who make it so. If you think about it, our thoughts are also unseen presences, similar to Nacha's gods. They are ideas that germinate silently within our hearts without anyone noticing. It's not until they emerge as a scream, demand, or a tree of resentment that others are alerted to their presence.

Everything that is planted bears fruit, so what is the point of sowing hate? Is it not absurd to fill with hate the heart of the person who will be tasked with caring for us in our old age, the person whom we will depend upon?

Why does mother insist that I label Rosaura's wedding invitations?

Today has been one of those days when I wish I had never been born. The only relatively good thing I can tell you is that I have been freed from the obligation of labelling the invitations. It was not an act of compassion towards me, but a realization that my terrible handwriting was ruining the envelopes. I've never had good handwriting. At school I was forced to write with my right hand because I was born left-handed. The teacher would often tie my left hand behind my back, and it made me hate calligraphy. I despise it. It's hard for me to write perfectly like my sisters do. Is a written message less important if the letters used to communicate it are uneven? I don't think so.
So after pointing out my errors and calling me clumsy, Mother ordered me back to the kitchen. I was relieved to return to my favorite place, but I was

so distraught that I burned my hand with boiling water. It happened because I have not been at peace for days now. I don't know where my head is.

Today Nacha gifted me a piece of heaven. She taught me a knitting stitch that only married women are allowed to use in her hometown. It looks like a climbing staircase. Nacha says that in her tradition it is believed that heaven can only be reached through family relationships. That is why unmarried women are not allowed to use this stitch because they don't know what it truly means to love a husband and children. Nacha's gesture moved me to tears, because I can never marry, but I can still reach heaven now that I know this stitch.

Nacha also taught me how to make an invisible knot. It is a simple but effective knot, truly unnoticeable that cannot come undone. I thought of Pedro. I don't know who tied our hearts together or for what reason, but I feel like our love is just as strong as this knot, even though he will no longer be my beloved and will soon become my brother in-law.

Invisible Knot

Take the first thread and put it over the one you wish to tie it to.
Cross under, and through the loop that was just made.
Do the same on the other side.
To finish, take the ends and pull. This creates the invisible knot.

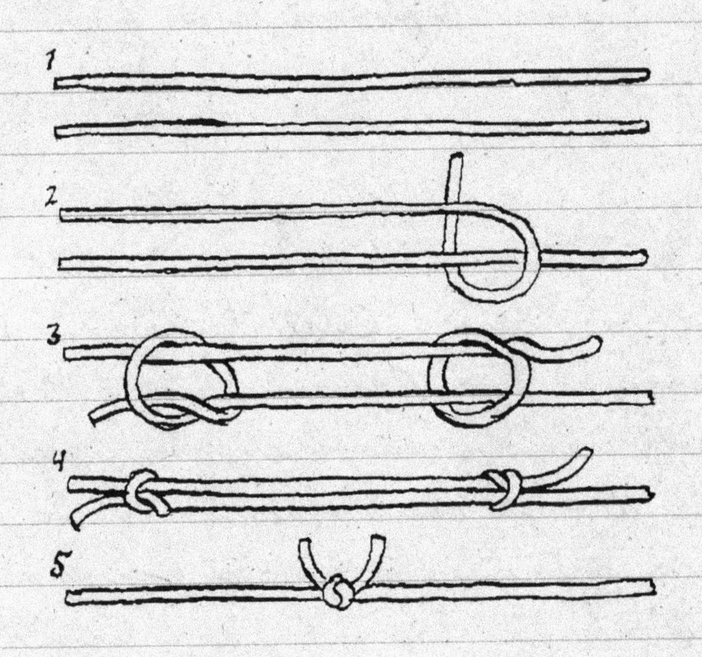

Today was Rosaura and Pedro's wedding. I behaved like a lady. The only moment that stood out was when I approached Pedro to congratulate him, he whispered in my ear that he had married my sister only to be near me. If the intention was to follow madness, I could have married his father to be near him! Would he have liked that? Of course not. Right? Who told Pedro that I would be pleased to see him marry my sister?

Anyway, today I felt a pain greater than anything Pedro's wedding could ever have caused. After the feast I discovered that Nacha had died. Her death leaves me completely abandoned and utterly alone. To make matters worse, mother accused me of putting an emetic in the cake to try and ruin the wedding. I have decided to make this diary a cookbook where I'll write down

the recipes and cooking secrets that Nacha taught me. Cooking will always be the best tribute to her, and the best way to keep her close to my heart.
This day brought a wedding and two deaths: of my dearest Nacha, and of Pedro as my beloved.

Miss

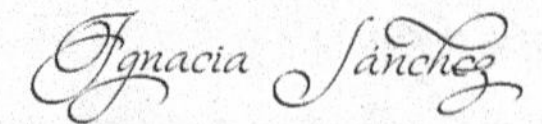

Passed, in the breast of the Holy Mother Catholic, Apostolic and Roman Church, at the age of 73.

With profound sorrow, the De la Garza Family shares this sad event, begging that you pray to God that her sould finds rest.

And invites you to the funeral that will take place today at 4 P.M. in the city cemetery.

Ciudad Porfirio Díaz, January 19th 1911.

MATER DOLOROSA.

Chabela Wedding Cake

Ingredients for Bread:

175 grams sugar

300 grams thrice-sifted flour

17 eggs

Lime zest

Ingredients for filling:

150 grams apricot paste

150 grams sugar

Ingredients for icing:

800 grams sugar

60 drops of lime juice and enough water to soak the sugar in

Ingredients for nougat:

10 egg whites

500 grams sugar

Instructions:

Cake:

Place 5 egg yolks, 4 whole eggs and sugar in a large pan. Whip until thick, then add two more whole eggs. Continue whipping until it is thick again and add two more eggs, repeating this process until all eggs have been added by pairs. Add lemon zest with the final two eggs. When the batter is thick enough, stop whipping and add sifted flour little by little with a wooden spatula. Finally, coat the mold with butter and sprinkle with flour before filling it with the dough. Bake for thirty minutes.

Filling:

Put apricot paste in a pan, add sugar and place on the fire. Stir continuously until it looks like marmalade. Remove from fire and let stand before placing in the middle of the cake, which must have been cut beforehand.

Icing:

Put water and sugar in a pan and stir continuously over the fire, until it boils. Sift into another pan, put back on fire, and add the lime juice until you can form a small soft ball between your fingertips, cleaning the edges of the pan with a moist cloth to prevent the mixture from crystalizing. Once the desired texture is achieved, place in a new pan that has been sprayed with water, and let cool. Afterwards, whip with a wooden spatula until it takes on the texture of breadcrumbs. Before spreading on cake, add a tablespoon of milk and place on the fire again so it dissolves and then add a drop of red coloring and cover the top part of the cake.

Nougat:

Whip the egg whites with the sugar until it caramelizes, and use to cover the sides of the cake.

Dear diary: ~

Please forgive my silence. I couldn't write. I couldn't even think. I could barely breathe. Although it had been several months since Rosaura and Pedro's wedding, they had yet to use the nuptial sheet, and last night they did. I felt betrayed. Pedro had assured me on the day of the wedding that he was only marrying her to be close to me. In a way, I wanted to believe him. The illusion made me feel good. It was my revenge against my sister. But alas, they have consumed their marriage. And I had to wash the blood-stained nuptial sheet. Nacha would have done it, but since her passing I have become her heiress. And on days like this, it burdens me terribly. I cried all day. Thank God that in the morning, the last chapter of my serialized novel "The Beggar Princess" came, because I was able to use it as an excuse for my tears.

worried Pedro but today, under the pretext that it had been one year since I became the official cook at the ranch, he brought me a bouquet of roses. It was a scandal. Rosaura and I were in the sitting room, knitting garments for her soon to be born child. When she saw Pedro, she stormed out with tears in her eyes. Mother shot me one of her deathly glances and I had to leave the room immediately. Mother's expression screamed "throw away those roses!" but I couldn't bring myself to. Instead, I clutched the flowers against my bosom so tightly that the thorns made me bleed. Maybe that blood altered the rose petal sauce that I prepared to serve with some quails for lunch, but the combination was undoubtedly explosive.

I don't know for certain how the events transpired, but Gertrudis removed all her clothes, set the shower stall on fire and rode off with a revolutionary on the back of his horse, galloping away. All I can say is that today I cooked this recipe and Gertrudis ran away.

Quails in Rose Petal Sauce

Ingredients:

12 roses, preferably red
12 chestnuts
Two tablespoons butter
Two teaspoons cornstarch
Two drops rosewater
Two tablespoons honey
Two cloves garlic
6 quails
1 dragon fruit
aniseed

Instructions:

Carefully pluck the rose petals trying not to prick your fingers, because not only would that be painful, but the petals may get smeared with blood. This not only alters the flavor of the dish, it may also cause potentially dangerous chemical reactions. It's important to pluck the quails while dry, because if you dip them in boiling water first, this alters the flavor of the meat. After they have been plucked and cleaned, tie the legs so they maintain a graceful position while the quail is browned in butter, and sprinkle with salt and pepper to taste.

Once the petals have been plucked, grind in a molcajete along with the aniseed. The chestnuts are separately toasted on a comal, peeled and boiled in water. Then they should be pureed. Garlic is chopped finely and browned in butter; once golden you must add the chestnut puree, the ground dragon fruit, the honey, the rose petals and salt to taste. In order for the sauce to thicken, you can add two teaspoons of cornstarch. Finally, drip through a sieve and add two drops of rose essence, and only two, because if you add more you run the risk of the sauce being too odorous and overly flavored. Once the sauce is seasoned you remove it from the fire. The quails must only be dipped in this sauce for ten minutes, long enough to be impregnated with flavor, and then let dry. Serve on a large platter, pour on the sauce and garnish with a whole rose on top and petals on the sides. Alternately they can be served on individual plates so you don't run the risk of losing the delicate balance of the decoration upon serving.

I was never very good at math but I understand that the sum of one and one is not always two. For me, Pedro and Rosaura will always be two people that were joined out of convenience but never lost their individuality. When two people truly come together they lose that individuality and become one being, fused to the bone. Like when Pedro and I swore eternal love with our hands joined. I remember that day I couldn't tell the difference between my hand and his. It was only one hand. The same thing happens in a molcajete when you make a salsa. All the ingredients are made one. Every cook knows that wonderful things happen inside pots. There is love, there is union, there is fire and passion. Everything dissolves, everything is fused, everything is transformed. That is what I offer Pedro every morning, my love in the form of aromas, flavors and warmth. Who says that is not making love?

Today was unforgettable. At midday I delivered my nephew, Roberto! Rosaura and I were left alone at the ranch because mother and Chencha had left to get supplies for the birth, due to a scarcity of supplies in town because of the revolutionary struggles. Pedro had also left the ranch earlier in the morning to fetch Dr. Brown from Eagle Pass. The doctor's arrival was delayed due to a clash between federales and revolutionaries and suddenly I was the one in charge of my nephew's delivery. I have no words to express what I felt when he was born. No description could ever do it justice. All I can say is that this child has brought love back into my life. Everything that I felt my sister had stolen from me has been returned tenfold. What we experienced together was so beautifully intimate and profound that it will be in my memory forever. At first I was quite nervous. I didn't know how to assist in childbirth and if Rosaura had

any idea she couldn't communicate it to me. The pain took all her energy and concentration. I don't understand why at school we are taught so many useless things instead of things that help us live, to receive, honor and respect life. To get down on our knees and bless the mystery of life. That was what Rosaura and I did when we had the child in our arms.
I don't need to be the mother of Rosaura and Pedro's son to cry tears of joy over this child whom I feel is mine. Like he is my son too. It's like when I sow corn and beans. I feel that they are a part of me. They are my parents, they are my children. They are me and I am them.

Later in the afternoon I went to the garden and planted my nephew's umbilical cord in the shade of a tree. Nacha always taught me the importance of returning nourishment to nourishment. I tried to do it with great respect and invoking the presence and blessings of our

forebears with my chants and prayers. I remembered a poem that Nacha taught me, and I repeated it over and over. I hope I honored her tradition, I truly put my heart into it.
Nacha told me that not only should we thank the Earth that nourishes us and allows us to be born and grow on it, but we must also thank the heart of the sky. We all have an umbilical cord that connects us to it and the cosmos uses it to feed us. Since I first heard of this idea, I have not been able to stop thinking of the Milky Way. That must be the origin of the cosmic food that nourishes us. It is nice to know we can take root in the skies.
I'll try to remember this when the earth has nothing more to offer me.

There is nothing sadder than listening to a child cry of hunger. Roberto didn't stop his bawling all day. When Dr. Brown finally showed up he explained that Rosaura had a fit of eclampsia and was very close to dying. Due to her delicate health she would be unable to feed her child. We found a wet nurse in town that helped in a pinch but yesterday on her way to the ranch she was killed by a stray bullet. Cow's milk is not good for little Roberto because his tiny stomach is not yet completely developed. After hearing my nephew cry for hours I had the idea of offering him my dry breast, so he would at least be entertained. The child nursed with such strength that he managed to get milk out of me. Yes, it's true! I don't know how it's possible, but I now have milk to give him. Only Pedro is aware of this, and thanks to his cooperation I have been able to feed Roberto while keeping it a secret from mother, who suspects nothing.

Today was a strange day because for the first time in my life I saw a look in mother's eyes that I was unable to interpret. It was almost sweet.

We were leaving the market with the things we had just purchased to prepare the mole for Roberto's baptism when we ran into a mulatto man. He was walking with his wife and children. When mother saw him she stopped dead in her tracks. When the man saw mother, he stopped too. He bowed his head, removed his hat and said "My respects to you and your family Doña Elena. How is everyone?"

"Fine, thank you," answered mother, with a hoarse voice that sounded strangely embarrassed, as if it were sinful to speak to that man, and she picked up her pace. She hurriedly looked around to ensure no one had seen the exchange. Then she noticed me at her side, staring at her, and became cross.

"Stop looking at me like a fool and walk!" she shouted, and the moment was lost. Everything returned to normal.
I would like to understand why mother lives with so much anger in her heart.

Turkey mole with Almonds and Sesame

Ingredients:

1/4 of a mulatto chile	1/2 onion
3 pasilla chiles	Wine
3 ancho chiles	2 chocolate tablets
A fistful of almonds	Anise
A handful of sesame seeds	Lard
Turkey broth	Cloves
One biscuit	Cinnamon
Peanuts	Pepper
	Sugar
	Chile seeds
	Five garlic cloves

Instructions:

After the turkey has been dead for two days, clean it completely and boil with salt. Turkey meat is tasty, even delicious if the animal was fattened correctly. This is achieved by keeping the birds in clean pens with plenty of grain and water.

Fifteen days before the turkey is to be slaughtered, begin feeding it small nuts. One on the first day, two on the second day and so forth, no matter how much corn they consume voluntarily in that interval of time.

Toast the almonds and sesame seeds on the comal. Remove the veins from the ancho chiles, and toast them as well but not for too long lest they become bitter. This must be done in a separate pan, because you must add some lard. Then grind in the metate with the almonds and sesame seeds.

When the almonds and sesame seeds are finely ground they must be mixed with the broth the turkeys were boiled in and add salt to taste. Grind the clove, cinnamon, anise, and pepper in the metate, and finally also grind the biscuit which must have been previously fried in lard with the chopped onion and garlic.

Mix everything with the wine in a big clay pot. Add turkey meat, chocolate tablets and sugar to taste. Once it thickens it must be removed from the fire.

There's no doubt that mother's favorite expression, "By the time you go, I've already gone and come back," is very true. There is no keeping anything from her. During Roberto's baptism she did not stop staring at me with an unusual expression. Like she saw me but didn't see me at the same time. The light in her eyes seemed dim. I didn't care, as I was so happy. The mole was delicious, even mother liked it, which is saying something, because she can always find a defect in my cooking. It's too salty, or not salty enough, it is raw, or burned... In other words, she is a specialist at finding fault. For this reason it was quite flattering that she congratulated me on the mole because I cooked it all by myself. When we returned from the market she locked herself in her room and Chencha was too busy setting up the patio for the party. Well, the mole was delicious and all the guests enjoyed it. When it came time to feed Roberto, I asked Pedro to help me keep a lookout and I headed

for the pantry with the child in my arms.
I took advantage of the fact that mother was chatting with Father Ignacio.
I must confess I was overconfident.
Mother's eyes seemed lost in the horizon, which I attributed to her boring talk with Father Ignacio, so I calmly left the party. Once in the pantry, Roberto desperately latched onto my nipple and drank so much milk he immediately fell asleep in my arms. When this happened before, all I needed to do was take my nipple from his lips and he would immediately wake and continue feeding.
Thank God this time that technique didn't work, because the alternative was to cover my breast, put it back in my blouse and try to button up. It was easy enough to do with the breast Roberto fed on because it was empty and soft, but the other one as still solid as a rock and full of milk. It was complicated for me to fit it back in my blouse. It

sprayed milk as soon as I touched it. I was trying to keep it under control when Pedro came in to help me. His eyes were wide with terror. In spite of that, when we managed to cover my breast, Pedro couldn't help but to clean the dripping milk from my skin with his fingers and then lick them in a way that seemed lustful and out of place.

And then we heard mother's hurried steps as she approached and hastily flung the door open. I can't thank the heavens enough that we had just enough time for her to find me completely covered and Pedro holding Roberto in his arms.

I always kept a bottle near to maintain the illusion that the child fed from it. But under mother's penetrating gaze nothing remained hidden. She frowned in disapprocal, turned and left. In the evening when all the guests had left she surprised everyone by suggesting to Pedro and Rosaura that they move to San Antonio, arguing that the revolution was getting more dangerous and she didn't want them to be in danger. I was impressed by the speed with which she planned everything. She said Pedro and Rosaura could stay with relatives in the city while they found a place to rent, and Pedro could work as an accountant in one of mother's cousins' businesses.

Señor, no lo que yo sino lo que tú
no cuando yo, sino cuando tú
porque no mando yo, si no
mandas tú.

Baptism of the child

Roberto Alonso
Múzquiz De la Garza

Chapel of San Labrador
Piedras Negras, Coah.
By the hand of
Father Manuel Guerra

His Godparents:
Jorge Muzquiz Castillos
y Ma. Cristina Estrada
De Muzquiz

Piedras Negras
(antes Ciudad Porfirio Díaz), Coah.
18 de Marzo de 1912.

From a young age I learned to smell danger in the kitchen. I know perfectly well when a fire must be put out or fanned, but I am completely ignorant when dealing with human bodies. I see the fire rising and do nothing to control it even though we are under mother's constant vigilance. She doesn't take her eyes off us for an instant, yet Pedro and I have been carrying on for days, brushing our bodies together when we pass each other in the hall, or touching knees under the table more and more frequently. But last night we went too far and I heard an alarm inside my head. It was so hot that mother decided we should all sleep in the hammocks outside. At midnight I had an urge to use the commode and I ran into Pedro who was eating chilled watermelon. Pedro whisked me off into a corner and we kissed and touched each other desperately. I can still taste the watermelon on my lips.

I don't know what would have happened if I hadn't heard mother calling me. I wonder if she really needed me to fetch her fan, or if she suspected that Pedro and I were together. So as not to arouse suspicions, I returned immediately to my hammock and held my urge to pee all night... and all night I craved more watermelon.

It was all for nothing. Mother, who seemed to have forgotten about her San Antonio idea, got back on track and wants Rosaura and Pedro to leave the house in a few days.

The last image I have of Roberto is a dark dot in the middle of the dust raised by the carriage he and his parents rode away in. I stood at the doorway until he was completely gone from my sight. The dust whirlwind they left behind, the shound of the horses galloping away, the child's wailing, the pain in my breasts and my milk dripping on the soil will forever be etched in my memory. I'll write just these few lines and then remain silent. The cold is unbearable. My inner fire has been snuffed out suddenly. I am no longer a provider of heat.

I shall say good-bye for a while, dear diary. I am running out of words. The only ones I wish to keep are these words that Pedro wrote in this note he gave me as he said good-bye. I repeat them over and again like a prayer, not to remember the cowardly

Pedro but so that Roberto may hear me and know that I am with him, I am with him, I am with him.

I will go away, but I will never leave you. I remain in the water, in the wind, in the amber of dusk. I will go away, but remember that I will never, ever leave you.

Chorizo Sausage

Ingredients:

8 kilograms of pork loin
2 kilograms pork head or scraps
1 kilogram ancho chiles
60 grams cumin
60 grams orégano
30 grams pepper
60 grams clove
2 cups garlic
2 liters of apple vinegar
1/4 kilograms salt

Instructions:

Pour the vinegar into a pot and place it on the fire, then add the chiles from which you have previously removed the seeds. As soon as it boils, remove from the fire and cover pot so the chiles become soft. Grind the spices along with the chiles in the metate. To make this easier it helps to add a small splash of vinegar or two while you grind. Finally, mix the finely chopped or ground meat with the chiles and spices and let stand for a long time, preferably overnight. Once sufficient time has passed, fill the tripe casings. They must be clean and cured beef tripe. Use a funnel to fill. Tie the tripe every four fingers of length and pinch with a needle to let air out, which could otherwise damage the chorizo. It's important to compress the filling very well to leave no space

Sometimes I truly admire mother's capacity to control, dominate and intimidate. One glance from her is sufficient to subdue even the bravest man. A few days ago some revolutionaries came by the ranch looking for food and mother defended the ranch very bravely. Nicolás had left to buy cattle with two other workers. Rosalio and Guadalupe, the two workers that remained, stood by mother when the troop arrived. They say there was a very dangerous moment when the rebels tried to enter the pantry to look for supplies and mother stopped them at gunpoint. She said they could take anything they wanted from the granary and the corrals but they would not step foot in her house. That was because Chencha, a pig and I were hidden in the basement and mother didn't want them to find us. Before the revolutionaries arrived, mother had hidden away her most prized possessions. Yes, the pig was in the same category as Chencha and I. Its flesh was as valuable as ours, because it was her last remaining animal and she planned to make it into chorizo sausages. Chencha was our last cleaning maid and I, well, I am supposed to care for her until she dies. Before we went into the basement Chencha and I helped mother kill some chickens. We stuffed them with grains and buried them in ashes inside clay pots so they wouldn't be taken too. That keeps them fresh for a week. Everything went well in spite of mother shooting the few chickens the revolutionaries found, just to prove who was in charge. When that happened, the troop captain and mother stared each other down, their fingers steady on their triggers. Rosalio says that the captain averted his gaze first and ordered his troops not to shoot. I must confess that from my hiding spot I wished from the very bottom of my heart that mother would be killed so I could be free. It hurts me so to have these thoughts!

Oxtail Soup

Ingredients:

Two oxtails
One onion
Two garlic cloves
Four tomatoes
1/4 kilogram green
beans
Two potatoes
Four morita chiles

Instructions:

Chop oxtails and boil in water with a piece of onion, a garlic clove, and salt and pepper to taste. It's convenient to add more water than usual because we will be making soup, and any good soup must be watery enough without being watered-down. The rest of the onion and garlic are finely chopped and fried in a pan. Once golden, add chopped potatoes, green beans, and tomato until seasoned. Pour this into the pot where the now cooked oxtails are. Let all ingredients boil in unison for half an hour. Remove from the fire and serve very hot.

This recipe returned my soul to my body, and here I am writing again. Chencha speaks the truth when she claims that a good soup can cure any physical or mental malady. I had been beside myself since I learned of Roberto's death. I can't seem to recall anything of the day that mother called Dr. Brown to put me away in a madhouse. The only thing I am sure of is that when I learned of my nephew's passing I yelled at the top of my lungs that it was mother's fault and as a response I received a blow with a wooden ladle that broke my nose. After that I must have lost my mind because I don't recall a thing. I don't know how long I spent stowed away in the pigeon loft. Up there everything was dark, as black as night, until a pair of deep blue eyes appeared to rescue me. Eyes that looked like two pools of water. Eyes that sheltered and protected my nude body.

These ocean eyes belonged to John Brown who wrapped me in his coat, led me down from the pigeon loft, put me in his wagon and brought me to his house instead of the madhouse. It has been several months since that fortunate day. To live in this house has been a gift, the best thing that has ever happened to me. But it wasn't until today, after Chencha brought me this oxtail soup that I was able to completely reconnect with my soul. The very first sip brought forth all the aromas and flavors of Nacha's kitchen, that admirable woman who didn't need to be my mother to lovingly feed me, instead of my real mother who only ever used a spoon to break my nose. As I ate my soup, Chencha babbled incessantly. She got me caught up on everything. Her mouth did not stop. Chencha's verbosity is astounding. When she begins to talk she runs on and on, like a loose thread in pantyhose. When I finished my soup I asked Chencha to tell mother that I intended never to return home.

Then we said good-bye. I cried a lot as I hugged Chencha, but they were tears of liberation and healing. How I bless Chencha for her visit. Among other things she brought me you, Dear Diary. She said that as soon as I left the house she ran into my room and fetched you so mother would never read you. She worried that mother would learn of sesnitive matters.
I was so glad to have you back that I didn't stop to think that if Chencha knew about your content it was because surely she had read it herself, cover to cover. I was not cross, on the contrary, it amused me. No wonder the gossipy Chencha had made such an effort to learn to read and write when she learned that I kept a diary!

Last night I slept like a log. It was such a relief to tell mother I would never come home! I also enjoyed the silence in my room when Chencha had left. Chencha is adorable, but she talks too much! I'm not saying our talk annoyed me, but it did rattle me. I had gone for so many days without talking to anyone that the sound was too much for my ears. Silence had been my only companion during my recovery. I refused to talk. There was no other way for me to express my grief. I couldn't find any words to do so. I didn't want to see, hear or do anything. I only wanted to sleep and sleep and sleep and hoped to never wake, because I felt this world had nothing to offer me but pain. But I also felt that I wasn't ready to die just

yet, I hoped that while my eyes were closed I might find inside of me some image, sound or memory to bring me back to life. I wanted to find some sort of inner book where I could read myself, understand myself, comfort myself. The only thing I was sure of was that I did not want to be mother's caretaker. I did not want to obey her orders for the rest of my life. I don't want to remember Roberto's death either. These were the only thoughts that occupied my mind during my waking hours. I seemed to forget while I slept, but as soon as I opened my eyes the first thing that came to mind was the child that starved to death because I wasn't allowed to feed him.

Found in John's garden.

I think that my desire to both inhabit and leave my body, to die and live at the same time, took me to another place. It was some sort of journey or dream, something I can't describe.

I had experienced something similar before, as a young girl. I learned to stand next to mother for long hours at a time without really being there. My mind traveled to other places until the phrase "Do you understand girl?" brought my senses back to mother's complete and utter service. But at John's house it's been different. I realized it was happening when I was sitting next to a Kickapoo woman with whom I usually have tea, but suddenly when John entered the room she disappeared. I was alarmed! I thought that maybe mother was correct and I had gone mad, but not a single word escaped my lips. I asked nothing. I let John be the one to speak. I enjoy listening to him talk. One morning in his company can teach me me more than all my years of grade-school. I continued knitting like nothing had happened. John was surrounded by test-tubes and strange scientific apparatuses. I have no clue what he was up to. He looked up and asked me "How goes your chrysalis?" referring to the enormous bedspread I was knitting. I shrugged for an answer. John smiled and continued working. I like the way that John respects my silence. I will never run out of gratitude for it. I continued knitting while I inconspicuously searched for the Kickapoo woman with my eyes. Then I saw her in a picture on the wall. John noticed, and asked "Do you like the picture? It's my grandmother. Her name was Morning Light. She was a Kickapoo Indian who knew a lot about plants and their healing powers. Of course, my grandfather's family had a very hard time accepting her, it took them many years. They found her quite strange, a

savage of sorts. Until finally, one by one she cured their ailments, and they learned to love her tremendously.
This room was her favorite, and here she prepared her teas. That is why I set up my lab in here."
John took the picture off the wall and placed it in my hands. I was very surprised to see that it was dated 1847! How was it possible for me to spend so much time with a woman who had passed away before I was born? I don't know. The only thing that's certain is that she taught me how to listen to silence.

Dr. John Brown

Today I headed to John's laboratory again, knowing full well that I wouldn't see Morning Light any more. I found John making matches and as usual, when confronted with my silence, he spoke. First he told me about Brandt, a chemist who sought the philosopher's stone by fusing urine with a metal extract. He failed in his quest, but instead of finding a magical way to make gold, he discovered phosphorous, a luminous element that burns quite vivaciously. He told me that this element was originally obtained by calcining the residue of urine after it has evaporated, but it is now extracted from animal bones that are rich in phosphoric acid and lime. Then he said that since we all have bones and urine, we all possess within us the necessary elements to produce phosphorus. Later on I observed him carry out an experiment with phosphorus, mercury and a candle. First he melted the phosphorus and the mercury in a crystal tube with the flame from the candle, then using a flask he added oxygen slowly. When the oxygen met the melted phosphorus it lit up in a flash and blinded me. I would have never thought that matches were made this way. You buy a box at the market and that's that, without understanding all the steps necessary to make them. I loved what I learned at the laboratory today, but my favorite part was a theory that belonged to Morning Light. John told me that his grandmother was convinced that we are all born with a box of matches inside us, but we can't light them on our own. We need the help of a candle and oxygen, as the experiment had proved. Oxygen can come from the breath of a person we love, and the candle can be any food, music, a soft caress, or a word that strikes one of our matches. That makes us feel a rush of emotion and an intense heat that dissipates in time. That heat fills our soul with energy. That combustion is its nourishment. If a person does not find the detonators for their box of matches in time, the box will dampen and the matches will no longer have the capacity to ignite. John's words made me think deeply. I fear that my box of matches is irreversibly dampened.

A recipe for making matches

Ingredients:

1 ounce powdered potassium nitrate

½ ounce minium

½ ounce powdered gum arabic

1 dram phosphorus

saffron

cardboard

Instructions:

Dissolve the gum arabic in hot water until it becomes a not quite thick liquid. When it is ready, add phosphorous and dissolve, as well as the potassium nitrate. Then add enough minium to give it color.

Once the paste is ready, prepare the cardboard for the matches. Dissolve an ounce of nitrate in a liter of water and add a bit of saffron for color. Bathe the cardboard in this solution. When it is dry, cut it in small strips and add a bit of paste to the tips. Bury them in sand and let them dry

Little by little my voice has been returning. Now I feel an urge to leave my room, to speak to John, to play with his son, to become part of the daily lives of this peaceful and loving family.
I have also learned that my hands can do and make so many things. Waiting on mother was one of the things I could do, but now that I don't live for her, that I'm free, I have learned new recipes and new knitting stitches. Unlimited and unrestricted. At mother's side there were only two ways to do something: right or wrong. My activities were limited to her approval or disapproval. Now I know that there is also a "maybe," a "why not?," a "let's try" or a "what if?" That might be the reason why I love to knit even though there are only two stitches to be used, they allow you to invent a myriad of different combinations. The same thing applies to the kitchen. It's

a shame that mother only accepted one way to cook every dish. There was no opportunity to rehearse new flavors or combinations. The recipe had to be respected no matter what. Caty, John's cook, has taught me new recipes. Today I learned how to make San Antonio Chili, a dish that John and his young son Alex greatly enjoy. I found it pleasant, nothing more. I guess I have to become accustomed to these new flavors. What's important is that we chatted and laughed during the meal. John was pleased with my cooking. He told me that the first time he tried this dish was at the Chicago World's fair, where he also met Tesla, the scientist he admires most. He said that my version was better. When dinner was over, John took my hands and thanked me for cooking. I discovered that I enjoyed feeling his skin upon mine. Maybe I am beginning to feel something other that pure gratitude for John.

San Antonio Chili

Ingredients:

2 lbs beef shoulder chopped in half inch cubes

1 lb pork shoulder chopped in half inch cubes

1/4 cup lard

1/4 cup pork fat

3 medium onions, chopped

6 garlic cloves, finely chopped

1 liter water

4 ancho chiles

1 serrano chile

6 dry red chiles

1 tablespoon recently ground cumin seeds

2 tablespoons oregano

Salt to taste

Instructions:

Sprinkle a bit of flour on the beef and pork cubes before frying. Sauté briefly at high heat. Add onion and garlic and cook with meat until onions are golden. Add water and let sit on low heat while the chiles are prepared. Remove veins and seeds from chiles, then chop finely. Grind them in a molcajete with oregano and salt. Add this mix to the meat and let it cook on low heat for two more hours. When the lard becomes a froth, remove from fire and get rid of excess fat.

Last night I was observing this picture my sisters and I. It's one of the few things Chencha brought me along with you, Dear Diary. It was taken at a fair. I like it because it looks like I'm sitting on the moon. As a child I liked to pretend that the cardboard moon was real. This memory made me feel melancholy and a couple of tears escaped my eyes. At that moment John was passing by and he asked me if something was wrong. I told him no, but he saw the picture in my hands and asked "do you miss your sisters?". I answered "Yes, but it's not so much the nostalgia as it is the feeling of thinking that the sky that's behind us in the picture is something I will never be able to see again". John's only answer was "throw your bedspread over your shoulders, we are going out." We got on his carriage and set forth on a road that led us outside of town for a few kilometers. It was a cloudless night, the sky covered in stars. I thought, "What did we

come all the way out here for? We could have seen the same stars from the garden at his house." Well, maybe not so many, and not as bright, but many nonetheless.
I decided to not complain or ask anything. John asked me to sit down and we did so on my bedspread. Suddenly, a meteor shower began. I have never seen anything so beautiful in my life. I looked at John as he told me with a wink in his eye: "An astronomer friend of mine told me of this event." We both remained silent and enjoyed the spectacle. The sky rained upon us and it moved me to tears. John held me in his arms to comfort me and unexpectedly kissed me. At that moment I didn't know if John's kiss lifted me to the sky or brought the sky down to the ground for me. I saw bright flashes of light inside me even though my eyes were closed. I recovered the fake cardboard sky of this old picture a hundredfold, and I understood that Nacha was wrong, that there are many different

ways to reach heaven. On the ride back home, with our hands joined, John explained that we can never lose the sky, as it is inside of us. All of the atoms that form our body were once created in the heart of the stars. He reminded me of the matches and phosphorous experiment. He spoke to me of carbon, hydrogen and many other things but I didn't pay much attention to his words because internally I was still celebrating that my matchbox wasn't irreversibly dampened! On that starry, luminous and loving night, John struck many matches with his kiss. I even feared that my entire box might be ignited all at once like Morning Light had warned John once. She told him that if a powerful emotion should have this effect, then a brilliant tunnel would appear before our eyes, a tunnel that separates us from the other world, and we might be tempted to cross it. Fortunately that didn't happen. Last night there was no need for John to declare his love or for me to accept it. Those formalities were eclipsed by the explosion of light that enveloped us.

Dear Diary, please don't consider me ungrateful. It's true that when I am very happy I abandon you, and I only return to lay my sorrows on you. But that is life. I'm truly sorry. I haven't written anything since the meteor shower! I will try to get you up to date. The morning after that unforgettable night I spoke to John because I did not think it proper to live under his roof after the kiss we shared, lest it be repeated. I told him I would find a place to live and find work as a cook somewhere. John laughed, and said he did not think it a pressing matter and would not allow it. We spoke at length. He told me that since his wife's death he hadn't felt a love as profound as the one he felt for me now. To make matters brief, he proposed marriage. He said the last thing he wanted was to expose me to gossip so he recommended a speedy wedding. Of course I said yes! I'm very happy at his side. Of course I also warned him about facing

mother's resistance to our wedding. John trusts he can convince her by fair means. I doubt it, and so we shall investigate the legal age for marriage according to the Civic Code in Mexico. I understand that men are allowed to marry at 14 and women at 12 if they have their parents' permission. Without that permission both men and women must wait until they are 21. I am about to turn 18 so I would have to wait three more years. An eternity!
Our plans are serious enough that John has spoken to his son Alex about it.
The boy is content with the news. We get along wonderfully. We have spent many hours playing and cooking together.
At first I tried to not become too attached to another child that wasn't my own, but now that I am marrying his father I have opened my heart to him without fear and the child responded in kind. But just now that I am so happy and everything is going well, Nicolas,

one of the workers at the ranch, came to see me to tell me that the same day that Chencha had come to visit me, as soon as she had returned to the ranch some bandidos had attacked. Chencha was raped and mother was beaten so badly that she was paralyzed from the waist down. When our nearest neighbor Paquita Lobo heard of the attack she suggested I be fetched but mother opposed the idea vehemently. She said she wanted nothing to do with me. As the days passed Nicolas thought it better to tell me of the events because there was no one else but me who could tend to mother and be up to her standards. I imagine the truth is that no one else could withstand her abuse.

I was deeply affected by this news. Any dignified person would have immediately rushed to their mother's aid, but that wasn't my case and I no longer know what to think of myself. It took me a while to speak to John of this and together we decided that I'll return to the ranch. John offered to take me and to look after mother as a medical doctor as well. Dear Lord I beg you to please give me the strength I need.

To be honest, I have not missed mother, much less waiting on her, these past few months. I never missed cooking or ironing for her, bathing her or brushing her hair. Now that I am forced to do it again I realize that there is a part of domestic work that gives me pleasure. What I reject now and forever is work done out of obligation. Not the rest. I like to rise early, go to the market and walk among the vendors, smell the fruit and vegetables, to be seduced by them and plan what I'll cook depending on my craving and desire. I like to touch vegetables with my hands, weigh them, caress them and listen to them. I feel like they speak to me, like they say "I still need two days to be ripe enough" or "my time is over, put me back in the ground" or "I would love it if you served me with onions and nopal cactus." I like to buy flowers and place them on the table. I like to buy candles and light them when the time comes. I like to set the table with a tablecloth that I have embroidered and ironed myself. I like harmony, beauty and cleanliness. I enjoy when my kitchen, my bedroom, my bedside table, even my bedpan become temples where I share my time with others as well as accounts of what I have done with my time. I like to sing while I wash the laundry. I like to dance while I sweep. And I like to remain silent when I knit, embroider, and fray, because when I do so, stitch by stitch my soul is joined with another spirit as if they were threads. I don't know what John and his scientist friends would call it but it is a sort of divine energy that is ever present and that gives me peace and nourishes me. That's why I don't like people who sit down to eat and don't appreciate the fresh flowers that were placed, or overlook the care you have put in preparing their food. Basically, I don't like mother. I don't know if she missed me before her accident, but when we first saw each other again I noticed that she seemed glad to see me but had to swallow her pride so as to not kick me out of the house again. There we were, staring at each other face to face after so long and for the first time in my life it was mother who averted her gaze first. I am not the same Tita I was and maybe my cooking is different because mother immediately complained and said my cooking was bitter. As usual, I was at a loss of words. I even thought that since I had not cooked for so long my hands lost their impregnated smell of onions and that was a factor that had affected my seasoning, but then I forgot this idea because mother was the only one who complained about the flavor of the food I prepared. Chencha was very grateful for my return to the kitchen and said that my soups healed her more than any medicine. I'm glad to be able to help and console Chencha because she arrived to the ranch at a very young age and has never had a day's rest.

Chencha watering my crops.

Dear Diary,
Mother passed away today. First I felt relief, then I felt guilt and now I only feel grief. I don't understand what happened. She deteriorated very rapidly. First she had the idea that I was poisoning her. She demanded that Chencha cook instead. Chencha couldn't handle the verbal abuse and she went back to her hometown. Then we had a series of cooks that didn't last for more than a week each. Mother would dismiss them for any number of reasons. Finally I was the only one left to cook and wait on her. She continued to insist that the food had a bitter flavor caused by whatever poison I was putting in it. She began to drink ipecac syrup that she said counteracted the effects of my poison and that was what finally caused her death. It's such a potent emetic that it can prove fatal when taken in excess. I must say goodbye now, as I have to plan for the funeral. Fortunately John is by my side lending his support.

It is very hard for me to imagine mother hugging and kissing father, much less making love to another man. And it's positively puzzling to try to think of her as a woman so in love that she would have been willing to give up everything to run away with that man. A mulatto man, rejected by her family, a man she had been forbidden to marry in her youth, but later bore his child when she was married to my father.

How difficult.

In a few short hours the history of my family as I knew it has come crumbling down. I discovered that the truth was not true. In one second mother ceased to be the villain of the story in order to become a sad princess. The beggar princess, the character from my dear novels with whom I have identified so.

When I was dressing mother for her funeral I discovered that under her nightgown she kept a key inside a heart-shaped locket that hung on a chain around her neck. It was the key to her treasure box. I couldn't resist and I ran to unlock it. I knew where she kept it since I was a child, always in the back of her dresser. Inside the box I found pictures and secret letters between mother and Jose Treviño, as well as a small diary. I read it and discovered that Gertrudis is this man's daughter and not my father's. When she learned of her pregnancy, mother and Jose made plans to flee. But the night they were to run away together Jose was seriously wounded in an ambush. Aunt Cuquita, one of mother's sisters, told her Jose had died. I can only imagine the grief mother felt at hearing this news. Worse still, it wasn't true; mother was deliberately lied to. Jose's death had been ordered, but he managed to escape with his life. The instigators of this attack were my grandfather and Uncle Rafael, and the executors were two ranch workers who

threw Jose's body over the border thinking he was dead.
Mother learned the truth about everything from her friend Paquita Lobo, who couldn't keep the secret she had heard firsthand from Aunt Cuquita. Paquita couldn't handle seeing mother suffer so. But the truth came too late, after Gertrudis was born. Around that time Jose came back. He would not give up. He stayed away from the city for a while but returned three years later with the clear intention of taking mother with him. Mother and Jose met in secret a few times. They made plans to run away, plans that obviously never came to fruition. That was the last thing she wrote in her diary. Everything becomes confusing after that. I don't know what happened. I don't understand why mother, being such a strong-willed woman, didn't run away with him. Maybe she was pregnant with me already? I can't think of any other impediment. Anything I can conjure in my mind is pure speculation,

there is nothing in the diary but blank pages. It was as if mother's soul had died inside her body. What happened to Jose? I imagine he finally left town for some reason. Then again, he was probably the same man we ran into at the market before Roberto's baptism. I have many questions that no one can answer. Like for example: Did mother never speak to her sister Cuquita again because she was the one who told her the lie about Jose being dead? I never even knew I had an Aunt Cuquita until this day, when she showed up to the wake with Uncle Rafael, also previously unknown to me. If mother had the strength to cut off all her family relationships, why didn't she have the strength to run away with the love of her life? My last question is: Did mother name me Josefa in Jose's honor? That is likely, as she is the only one who often called me Josefita, when everyone has always just called me Tita.

Today, near the end of the wake, Pedro and Rosaura arrived for mother's funeral. They arrived in time to thank our neighbors for coming. Rosaura has a huge pregnant belly and Pedro seems tremendously sad. It hurt me to see in his eyes the gaze of a defeated man who has never been in charge of his own will. Or maybe it's just the face of a man who watched his infant son die. It was painful to see them arrive without Roberto. Pedro and I had not seen each other since they left years ago. Now he returned with empty arms, childless. When he embraced me to express his condolences I felt my body vibrate as before, which unnerved me. Pedro does not deserve my affections and John does not deserve me having those kinds of feelings for anyone else. I felt afraid to live close to Pedro again. I felt nauseous. My stomach felt a strange premonition of sorts. Rosaura saved me from dwelling on my emotions because she began her labor early, maybe from the stress of the trip or maybe from the shock of seeing mother's corpse. Fortunately John was around this time to properly deliver the child. It was a complicated procedure because Rosaura's placenta had rooted in her uterus and would not come loose. John had to make an emergency surgical intervention. Later on he explained to me how dangerous this situation can be because if an unexperienced person notices that the placenta is not coming loose they may pull on the umbilical cord and cause the uterus itself to fall out. Thank God this didn't happen, but even so, Rosaura cannot have any more children. I think that the beautiful girl Rosaura gave birth to somehow knew she would be the youngest and only daughter my sister would have and would be prohibited from marrying to care for her mother until her death, and that was why she tried to put down roots in the uterus.

In the midst of the commotion of my niece's birth I forgot to tell you that while Pedro and I waited in the sitting room to know if Rosaura was all right, he told me "You have changed a lot Miss Tita." and I answered "Maybe it's because now I do what I want and not what I'm ordered." I said this scornfully and Pedro realized it. I regretted saying so even before I finished speaking the words, although I did intend to make Pedro feel bad because I am still mad at him. Pedro lowered his head and kept silent for the rest of our wait. When John came out with the girl in his arms and gave her to Pedro to hold, Pedro cried a few tears. Seeing that stirred something inside me, I couldn't help it.

Pedro brought me this photograph,
the last image of Roberto.

I haven't slept well since Rosaura and Pedro returned to the ranch. The creaking of the wooden floors in Pedro's bedroom keep me up. Ever since Pedro found out that I am to marry John, he paces to and fro inside his room like a caged lion. Well, now he knows what it feels like. At least I can knit without bothering anyone, unlike him. Why doesn't he go for a walk outside? It's very inconsiderate to those of us who have to rest. The arrival of my niece Esperanza (that is to be her name, they wanted to name her Tita but I objected, I don't want that name to mark her for an unfair destiny) has me working double. Rosaura is still bedridden and I am the only one left to tend to her and the child. I don't want to make the same mistakes as with Roberto, so I am trying hard to get Rosaura to feed her own baby.

We are making great strides. Every day I make Rosaura a champurrado and that is helping her produce enough milk. But it is inconvenient because the child likes to sleep downstairs amidst the heat of the pots and pans but likes to feed upstairs with her mother, so I am climbing up and down stairs all day and I have to rub volcanic ointment on my legs every night.

Champurrado

Ingredients:

5 cups of water
1 cup cornmeal
1 chocolate tablet
1 cinnamon stick
brown sugar to taste

Instructions:

Boil 3 cups of water. The other 2 will be used to dissolve the cornmeal using a fork and trying to break up all lumps. Then sift this mixture into the boiling water. Let it boil for a couple of minutes more and then add the chocolate tablet in pieces, along with the cinnamon stick and the brown sugar. Let boil for 5 more minutes and remove from fire.

Pedro has finally stopped stomping around in his room. It seems that he understood that the rest of us find his insomnia very unpleasant.
He no longer paces to and fro, now he goes on horse rides at dawn.
He doesn't just ride, he gallops at full speed. When he returns he takes a cold bath and comes down for breakfast with a calm demeanor, yet reacts impatiently to any minor inconvenience. He cannot control his temper. He has become an explosive man who must make a great effort to behave properly. I feel guilty for this. I know how terrible he must feel. Jealousy is a true torment. As soon as I get the chance I will make him a cup of hot chocolate. When Nacha passed away I found amongst her belongings a recipe marked "for opening the heart" and it's nothing more than a cup of hot chocolate prepared ceremoniously and whipped to a special rhythm while chanting.

I have no idea about the melody or tempo but I'll give it my best effort. I'll repeat the phrases with all my heart hoping that Pedro can open his own heart and let go of all the pain and unhappiness he has locked inside.

I don't know how to even begin to write what transpired today. Maybe it's best if I follow the natural order of the events. I rose early, long before the roosters crowed, so I could have time make the mole for the champandongo. Tonight John will come to formally ask for my hand in marriage and I decided that this dish would be perfect for the occasion, because although its preparation is very time consuming it is a one-course meal that is served with rice and beans and that lessens the serving time.

It's strange to me that Rosaura, as my legal guardian, is now in charge of authorizing my marriage. Mother gave her this power until I come of age. Mother also named Rosaura executor of her will, so she will have to arrange all matters so I can receive my inheritance. But I am straying from the subject.

While the mole was cooking and the house was quiet because everyone still slept, I thought it would be the perfect time to prepare the ceremonial hot chocolate for Pedro. I didn't want him to become impatient and rude at dinner. I put the water on the fire and when it was about to boil I added the chocolate. I took special care to not let it come to a full boil and to grind the chocolate according to the special instructions of the ritual. The sun began to rise. I recalled that Nacha used to say that everything we do should be in accordance to the rhythm of the skies. It's very simple, the heavens tell us when to sow, when to reap, when the soil must rest, when it should be watered...Nature is wise, she said, we must listen to it carefully. So I asked the sun to help me learn the rhythm I should follow to whip the hot chocolate. I didn't want to be off, I wanted to whip with the heavens, I wanted the rhythm of my hands to reflect the pulse of the universe. I think the ceremony went well because when Pedro came down for breakfast I served him the hot chocolate and I observed how his face changed. His eyes began to sparkle like that day at church when I discovered love. When he finished drinking the chocolate he went outside to the garden, sat in the shadow of the apple tree and covered his face with his hands. I imagine he was crying, letting all his pain out. I didn't see him again until lunchtime when he tried to convince me to call off my wedding. I had been walking down the stairs with a potful of mole which I spilled everywhere. Pedro could not have chosen a worse time to try to speak to me. I yelled at him and told him he had no place to ask that of me after what he had done. Pedro tried to justify himself with the same old argument, that he married Rosaura to be near me, and I accused him of being a coward for not daring to steal me away. Well, I guess that whatever benefit came from the chocolate was erased in that instant. The argument ended with me trembling and him depressed. I felt unbearibly hot, like water for chocolate.

Fortunately we were interrupted by Chencha's return to the ranch. She was radiant. She had reconnected with her first suitor in her hometown and they had married. When she saw the state I was in, she sent me to rest and took over the kitchen. Later, when John arrived at dinnertime, Pedro tried to behave as best he could, which wasn't enough. On certain occasions he forgot the basic rules of etiquette that forbid political and religious talk at the dinner table. I was forced to brusquely change subjects so we could discuss my wedding instead of touchy subjects. John told Pedro and Rosaura that he would be leaving the next morning to fetch his only remaining aunt from the north of the United States so that she could be present at our wedding. When the compromise was sealed John gave me a beautiful diamond ring and I couldn't help but remember that earlier in the

day when I was bathing in the patio, Pedro stared at my naked body through the cracks between the boards. His gaze was fire, much brighter than the diamonds of my engagement ring.
I bid farewell to John with a long kiss. Alas, I felt a pit in my stomach. I was worried that he was going away for so long. I was afraid of being alone, I felt endangered.
I cleared the table with Chencha's help and when I went to store the dishes in the dark room I found Pedro waiting for me in the darkness. He closed the door with care and forcefully took me by the waist so he could kiss me. Tonight I lost my virginity to Pedro and I don't regret it. That is all I have to say.

Champandongo

Ingredients:

1/4 kilogram ground beef
1/4 kilogram ground pork
200 grams walnuts
200 grams almonds
candied citron
1 onion
2 tomatoes
sugar
1 liter cream
1 cup manchego cheese
1 liter mole
cumin
chicken stock
corn tortillas
oil

Instructions:

Chop onion finely and fry with the meat in a little bit of oil. While it's frying add cumin and a tablespoon of sugar. When the meat begins to brown, add chopped tomatoes along with the candied citron, and chopped pecans and almonds. When the meat is fully cooked and dry, fry the tortillas in oil, but not enough to harden them. In the container used to prepare the dish make a bed of tortillas, then cover with a layer of the meat and finally pour the mole over it. Cover with cheese and cream. Repeat these steps until the container is full. Place in oven and remove when cheese is melted. Serve with rice and beans.

Dear Diary,
remember how I said I had no regrets? Well, that was a lie. The guilt is killing me! I can't face Rosaura every day and pretend that there is nothing going on between Pedro and I. And what's worse is that she no longer considers me a competitor for her husband's affections since I am to marry John, so she sits in my kitchen all day trying to make conversation with me. She speaks about all sorts of private matters and I don't know what to say. It's even worse when she speaks to me of her intimacies. Rosaura says that Pedro hasn't touched her in months. She says he only impregnated her to have another child because he was very sorry to see her cry so, but not because he enjoyed the physical intimacy. My sister attributed Pedro's distance to her being overweight and has asked me to prepare a diet so she can lose the extra pounds she gained during her pregnancy. When she says these things

I feel the urge to look away. Rosaura would die if she knew that I can't keep Pedro's hands off me. Another thing that she thinks interferes in her relationship is her sudden halitosis. It breaks my heart to see her suffer, and more so because I consider myself responsible for her woes. I remember the day that John brought Alex to visit and the boy said he would like to marry Esperanza when they grew up. We all laughed, then froze when my sister said "My daughter can never marry because she must care for me until I die." Her words almost stopped my heart and I remember that when I cooked dinner that night I wished with all my heart that Rosaura's words would rot in her mouth. I don't know. Maybe it's the tremendous guilt that torments me and makes me feel like I am responsible for my sister's misfortune. What's incredible is that hearing Rosaura talk is like hearing mother talk. She thinks like her, has the same concepts of life that mother did, uses her same words, moves like her and sometimes even purses her mouth just like her. She is like a carbon copy of mother. I don't know how to explain it, but when Rosaura speaks I hear mother's voice coming from her mouth. It's curious because I have never been able to sing a duet with anyone because I can't follow a separate melody. Mother could do it very well and when I asked how she did it she said "it's easy, the orchestra is playing the second voice, can't you hear it?". No, I could never hear it, until now from my sister's mouth. Fortunately (or unfortunately because of the extra work) today Gertrudis returned to the ranch, just in time to have King's Cake and a foamy cup of hot chocolate. She arrived with her entire troop and escorted by Juan Alejandrez, the captain who stole her off on his horse. During the worst of the revolutionary fight they had lost contact but they found each other again and got married. I was very glad to see her so triumphant and happy. I am sure that her presence will make our daily life lighter, happier and more relaxed. It's a shame mother is no longer around to see her.

Hot Chocolate and Kings' Cake

Ingredients for chocolate:

2 lbs Soconusco cacao
2 lbs Maracaibo cacao
2 lbs Caracas cacao
4 to 6 lbs sugar
Oil

Instructions for chocolate:

The first step is to toast the cacao.
It's convenient to toast on a big tin plate instead of the comal because the oil released from the cacao beans can seep through the pores of the comal. When the cacao is completely toasted, clean using a sieve to separate the grain from the hull.
Preheat the metate by placing it in a big earthenware pot over the fire for a while.
When the metate is warm, remove it from fire and use to grind the cacao.
Mix with sugar. Then, separate the dough

with your hands, and form tablets in a long or round shape, whichever suits you. Let them stand in the open air. You may use the tip of a knife to make divisions in the tablets.

Ingredients for Kings' Cake:

30 grams fresh leavening
1 and 1/4 kilograms flour
8 eggs
1 teaspoon salt
2 tablespoons orange blossom water
1 and 1/2 cups milk
300 grams sugar
300 grams butter
250 grams candied fruit
1 small porcelain baby figurine

Instructions for Cake:

Mix the leavening in 1/4 kilogram of flour using your hands or a fork, and slowly add 1/2 of the warm milk.

When the ingredients are properly mixed, knead for a bit and let stand in the shape of a ball, until it grows to double its size. Use the rest of the flour to make a ring on the table and put the ingredients in the center. Begin kneading from the inside out, adding flour intermittently until you have added all of it. When the ball of dough and leavening has grown to double its original size, mix it with this new dough completely until you can separate it with your hands easily. Pick up any dough that has stuck to the table and integrate it as well. Pour the dough in a deep mold that has been previously greased. Cover with a napkin and wait for it to rise to twice its height again. Consider that dough takes about two hours to double in size and this must be repeated three times before it can be put in the oven. The second time the dough has doubled its size pour back on the table and shape into a strip. You may put some candied fruit inside if desired.

If not, just place the tiny figurine inside the dough wherever you wish. Now roll this strip, and join ends perfectly. Place on a tin plate that has been greased and sprinkled with flour, and shape into a doughnut leaving enough space around the edges because it will double in size once more. In the meantime light the oven to maintain a nice temperature in the kitchen. When the dough has doubled its size for the third time, decorate with candied fruit, glaze with a beaten egg and sprinkle with sugar. Put in the oven for twenty minutes and then let it cool.

I've never had a problem with food. I can enjoy any flavor, and hardly find anything disgusting. Quite the opposite from my sister Rosaura who is repulsed by any food that's new or different. Strangely, the last few days I have noticed an unpleasant, spoiled, fetid, acid taste in everything I eat. How is it possible that food that I have always liked is now making me nauseous? I'm getting desperate. I don't know if it's the food that disgusts me or if I disgust myself. What kind of person would give up the opportunity to marry John Brown? What kind of person would betray him? John is the closest thing to perfection I have ever known. I like to be with him. I like it when he holds me and kisses me. But alas, none of his embraces have made me feel what Pedro makes me feel. Of course that doesn't justify what I'm doing and I have no one to blame for my behavior but myself. I am the only one in charge of my actions.

It was easier when I had someone to obey. Well, at least I did not indulge in such folly and have to deal with this awful remorse. Now every waking hour I am plagued by catastrophic images.
I wake up nauseous and my breasts hurt, worrying symptoms of a pregnancy that would complicate everyone's lives.
I wonder if mother was tormented by similar thoughts, and if she suffered the same annoying and nauseating symptoms when she carried my sisters and I.
Undoubtedly carrying Gertrudis must have been the hardest of the three.
Of course, mother was in a better position than I am now. She was married, and although the child she was carrying was the product of infidelity, only she knew this fact. I'm not even married. How can I justify this pregnancy? How can I move ahead with the marriage I had planned?
Today, when I was making custard fritters for Gertrudis I had to make a great effort to suppress my nausea while I beat

the eggs. Gertrudis noticed. I broke down in tears and confessed everything. It was such a relief! Gertrudis listened to me, consoled and comforted me. She sees everything from a different perspective. In her opinion, the intruder is Rosaura. She was the one that came between Pedro and I, knowing about the profound love we shared. How I wish I could see the world like Gertrudis, and have the power of command she has. She does what she wants, when she wants and whenever she wants, without asking permission of anyone or regretting a thing. Men obey her orders without hesitation. There is no problem she can't solve, and she always gets her way.

As I was in no condition to make her fritters, she practically forced me out of the kitchen and sent me off to speak to Pedro about my pregnancy. I did so, knowing that I was leaving my sister abandoned in a realm she had no power over: the kitchen. But to my surprise

Gertrudis, despite not knowing how to cook at all, made Sergeant Treviño, one of her underlings, prepare the fritters while following my recipe! I don't know why that surprised me, honestly. If she was able to become a general and command a troop, why wouldn't she be able to handle some fritters, no matter how complicated the recipe may have seemed?

Custard Fritters

Ingredients:

One cup cream
6 eggs
Cinnamon
Simple syrup

Instructions:

Separate egg whites from the yolks. Mix yolks with the cup of cream and beat well until this mixture is light and fluffy. Pour in a casserole that has been previously greased with lard. This mixture must not be deeper than a finger. Heat on low fire and let it stand. Once the custard is cool chop in cubes, not too small so they may crack. Then whip the egg whites which will be used to dip the fritter in before it's fried in oil. Finally pour syrup on them and sprinkle with ground cinnamon.

Instructions for syrup

Beat an egg white in a quart of water for every 2 lbs of sugar, two egg whites in a quart of water for 5 lbs of sugar, or use the same proportion for larger or smaller quantities. Boil this syrup until it rises three times, calming the boil with a little bit of cold water which must be poured every time it rises. Remove from fire, let stand and remove foam.

Then add some more water with a piece of orange peel, aniseed and clove to taste and let boil once more.

Remove foam again and once it has reached the desired texture (you can make a tiny ball of it with your fingers), sift it. If you desire a more pure simple sugar like the kind used to sweeten liqueurs, after the previous steps you must decant it with the least movement possible.

Dear Diary,
yesterday was a hectic day. I will try to summarize what happened. I'd locked myself in my bedroom all afternoon because I didn't feel like talking to anyone. I had to mull over my conversation with Pedro. He was willing to leave Rosaura and Esperanza behind to run away with me, but I wasn't. There had to be a better solution for our problem, but try as I did, I couldn't think of one. In a very illogical manner, the person I most wanted by my side was the last person I wanted to see. To be at John's side would be the best and worst thing that could happen to me. His presence would immediately help me recover peace, but I would have to look into his stunning blue eyes and tell him I am pregnant with Pedro's child. Unavoidably, mother came to mind. How many nights must she have lost sleep over the same problem that troubles me now? To think of mother made me feel worse so I began to knit in order

to distract my mind. On other occasions knitting could clear my head immediately but last night it proved useless. It was Gertrudis' last night at the ranch and a party was organized with music and dancing. The noise was infernal. The laughing and singing was keeping me from the spiritual peace I longed for.
Suddenly I heard Pedro and Juan singing below my balcony. They were drunk. Almost at the same time I heard mother's voice in my head saying "See what you've done now? Pedro serenading you? Dear Lord! Take your things and leave this house before it's too late!"
When she was alive, I was never able to talk back to mother. The only time I tried, she broke my nose. But now that she was dead, I was able to talk back.
I snapped back and asked her to leave, to stop tormenting me. I didn't want to hear her anymore. She then accused me of indecency. I answered that I was only following her example, since she'd had a

bastard daughter herself. Our mental dialogue escalated into threats of eternal damnation until I could take it no more and told her to leave for ever, that I would not hear her anymore, that I hated her. These words shot out of my mouth like projectile vomit and I felt a great relief. My body and mind were so relaxed that I instantly felt how my period began to slide down from my womb slowly. I swear, I cried with relief. I wasn't pregnant!

I wanted to join the party to celebrate but just as I was coming down the stairs I heard screams below my window and I saw Pedro on fire and Gertrudis tearing off her skirt to use it to drown the flames. Later I was told that the accident was caused by a kerosene lamp that inexplicably exploded and rained fire down on Pedro. I rushed down the stairs and was by his side in seconds. Rosaura arrived at the same time. Pedro took my hand. I tried to pry loose from his grip to allow Rosaura her rightful place with her husband, but Pedro held on tightly and screamed for me to stay at his side. Rosaura turned and hurriedly left. I think I have lost her forever. I don't think she'll ever forgive such a public slight.

Dear Diary,
I'm now more confused than ever.
This is alarming, because as you well know, in the past I have been shaken up so bad that I couldn't speak let alone write, but this time my bewilderment is absolute. John returned to the ranch the day after Pedro's accident and as always his presence was a blessing. Despite being fatigued from such a long trip, John immediately took care of Pedro's burns with some tepezcohuite dressings that his grandmother had taught him. Pedro's recovery has been astonishing.
Since John returned from Pennsylvania we have seen each other every day but never in private, so we haven't had a chance to speak. He brought his Aunt Mary, who prudently let a week go by before coming to meet me. She didn't want her presence to interfere with Pedro's care and that was fortunate because Rosaura had locked herself in her room all week and it would have been awkward

to explain that situation to a guest.
Today Rosaura left her room and came to see me only to say that she did not intend to get a divorce but would also keep no further relationship of any kind with Pedro. She said I was free to do as I pleased. She only asks that we be discreet so she is not considered a fool in the eyes of society. What hurt me the most was that she forbid me to spend time with Esperanza because she doesn't want such a poor role model for her daughter.
I am not to bathe her, prepare her meals, or change her diapers. I am to have no contact with Esperanza.
I think John has noticed that something has gone horribly wrong in his absence but he has kept quiet. Of course he noticed that Rosaura has not been present for his medical visits nor has asked about her husband's health, and he is also aware of the palpable tension between me and Pedro. Still his mouth only opens to speak of pleasant things. I try to act normal

but he must have felt a difference in me from the very first hug we shared upon his return. I ran towards him and hugged him for a long time. I didn't want to budge an inch. I was sure that after my confession not only would our relationship change, but also the way we hug, the way we looked into our eyes cleanly, the way we share silence, the way we watch the sky. I never imagined how broad John's sensibility is, and how much he understands human beings.

I realized my error the night I prepared dinner for Aunt Mary. Despite all the setbacks in the kitchen while I cooked, as soon as we sat down everything went smoothly. Before we began to eat, I excused Pedro and Rosaura's absence. Aunt Mary greatly enjoyed the Tezcucana Beans I made and expressed it vehemently. There was only one obstacle to the conversation: Aunt Mary is quite deaf and can only read lips in English. John used this opportunity to speak to me in Spanish while his aunt was distracted eating. He asked me what was wrong. He expressed concern about our wedding being less than a week away, and he felt like I was hiding something. I tried to change the subject but John insisted and that was when I told him I couldn't marry him because I was no longer a virgin. While I said this I cried a couple of tears and Aunt Mary said it was beautiful to see a soon-to be bride cry from happiness. In order to prevent me from bawling, John took me by the hand and told me he didn't care about what had happened. He still intended to be my life partner. All he wanted to know is if I considered him so. If I did then we would marry in a week, if not, he would be the first to congratulate Pedro and ask him to give me the respect I deserve. Oh, how much grander did John's image become in my mind! And how much larger are my doubts about the decision I must make!

Beans with Chile Tezcucana Style

Ingredients:

Pinto beans
Pork
Pork rinds
Ancho chiles
Onion
Shredded cheese
Lettuce
Avocado
Radishes
Guero chiles
Olives

Instructions:

The beans must be first cooked with tequesquite and after they have been washed they must be cooked again with cubes of pork and chicharrón. After the chiles have been de-veined they must be soaked in hot water and finally ground. Chop the onion and fry in lard. Once it's brown add the ground chile and salt to taste. Once this sauce is seasoned, add beans, meat and chicharrón. When serving add shredded cheese as well as lettuce strips, avocado slices, chopped radish, guero chiles and olives.

Today was Esperanza's baptism.
I thought Rosaura would cancel it, but she didn't. All she did was put all party preparations on hold. Chencha asked me if she should comply. I said that if those were my sister's wishes we must respect them. Chencha asked many more questions, but I didn't satisfy her thirst for knowledge. In fact, since she returned to the ranch I have changed your hiding spot several times my Dear Diary, because inside your pages there is plenty of information I wouldn't want to share with anyone, much less Chencha, who might take sides between Rosaura and I and let her tongue run loose. I was surprised by Rosaura's decision but I understood perfectly that she wasn't in any mood to celebrate, especially for a baptism where I was supposed to be her daughter's godmother. How could she allow me to baptize Esperanza after asking me to stay away from the child? And how could I explain to John what was going on?

Rosaura was so grateful to him for saving her life when Esperanza was born, that she asked him to be godfather, and since we were to be married soon, I was asked to be godmother. Of course, that was before John left to get Aunt Mary and before Pedro and I had our encounters. How quickly did things change!
Now Rosaura treats me like a black sheep. I understand, in her place I would probably act accordingly. And if Esperanza was my daughter, I wouldn't want her near Rosaura, hearing ideas I don't agree with. In any case, to my surprise Rosaura organized a secret baptism. The party took place at the Muzquiz ranch. Rosaura didn't want me to cook and asked me to attend as a simple guest. That was fine by me, as I didn't have to work. Do you remember how she had refused to speak to me? Well, she is speaking to me again after she learned that John and I were effectively going to

marry and would not live at the ranch. Little by little she began to speak in short sentences to me, so at the baptism no one could notice that there was a problem between us. The only one who looked at me with disapproval was Father Ignacio. Rosaura must have told him something, or maybe it was because I have not been going to confession lately, or because I went to a different church... who knows? He made quite an emphasis during the liturgy where it is asked of the parents and the godparents if they renounce the devil. When he asked this question he looked directly at me with terrible eyes that made feel like a guilty sinner. And then the choir began to sing Ave María, which almost made me cry. That song has always awakened in me a sensation of purity. I loved to hear it as a child when I brought flowers to the Virgin. In those days I would even think I might like to become a nun. Now there is nothing left of that pure and innocent Tita, except for an image that remains in my memory. At the end of the ceremony Pedro and Rosaura commended their daughter to Our Lady of the Refuge, Virgin of the Sinners. I avoided meeting Pedro's gaze at all costs, because it was in front of that Virgin in that same church where we swore eternal love. I didn't want to feel his gaze on me. His eyes are my eternal perdition. I looked at John, because in his blue eyes I seek redemption.

I haven't slept for two days. My insomnia is caused by Pedro's intensified nightly pacing because of my imminent wedding, and because I have yet to finish my bridal gown. But in all truth, what is mostly keeping me awake at night is Esperanza's future. During the baptism I heard my sister tell Paquita Lobo that she would never allow Esperanza to marry. I am very worried that she hangs on to this ridiculous tradition and that I will not be around to fight it. I told John that I felt obligated to do something about it, but he advised me to not stick my nose in, that it's not the time. Many things can happen between now and when Esperanza is old enough to marry. He reminded me that we are her godparents and that we can lend our support when the time comes, and if she asks. He also reminded me that even though I'm leaving the ranch, I can stay involved in Esperanza's life. We're not moving to the other end of the world, only across the bridge. He's right, in a few days I will marry and soon will have children of my own. I will make sure they are not burdened by that stupid tradition. I have been spared from an unjust destiny, but a voice inside my head still asks, is it fair to only save oneself? What makes us think that we are not responsible for others' fates? For example, my sister Gertrudis is willing to give her life for others. I could do the same, but my revolution would consist of giving up my life, marriage and partner in order to stop a horrendous tradition from continuing. So I must decide to either marry John, be happy and forget about trying to save my family members, or stay single so I can prevent my sister from ruining Esperanza's life. If I leave, the tradition of the youngest daughter being prohibited from marrying will die out with me, but I won't be able to prevent it from continuing in Rosaura's family and

I wonder how many more generations this will affect. It's not enough that I refuse to perpetuate it, if it is to disappear completely then it must not be passed on to anyone anymore.

Today I might have made the worst mistake of my life. Time will tell. I rose early and bathed so Chencha would have time to braid my hair in a beautiful style that no one knows but her. When I was rinsing my hair with orange blossom water Pedro pried the bathroom door open and forced his way in. I shoved him and demanded that he leave immediately. With tears in his eyes, Pedro begged me not to marry John. He had already made this argument a few weeks ago when he asked me to not make the same mistake he did. Back then I told him I had the right to marry whomever I wanted and I thought he had understood this, but he obviously didn't, so I tried to be more forceful. I harshly accused him of being a selfish man who only considered his own comfort. What could he offer me? Fleeting moments, secret encounters, hidden love? John, on the contrary, offered me a clean, solid and free relationship. Well, Pedro didn't want to

hear any of it. He took me by the waist and kissed me passionately.
I don't know how but I was able to escape from his embrace. I ran to the house, got dressed and went for a walk. That was the only thing that could calm me. I was to marry John in a few short hours and I wanted my head to be clear. I walked, walked and walked and when I came to I realized I had crossed the Piedras Negras bridge and was now in Eagle Pass, standing in front of John's house, who was greatly surprised to see me from his window. He ran down and hugged me. I didn't have to say much, I only said that I couldn't marry him because I wasn't completely sure of my feelings.
After a painful silence John cleared his throat and asked me to give him a few minutes to remove his tuxedo and take me back to the ranch. I waited in his sitting room. Alex saw me and asked why I wasn't wearing my wedding gown. I burst into tears. Fortunately John came back

down, ruffled the boy's hair and told him that the wedding was cancelled, and he would explain later. I will never forget the boy's baffled expression. On our way back John and I stopped for a moment to agree upon the way we would go about with the cancellation. When we arrived to the ranch I went to my room to touch up. Chencha was worried because I had been gone for so long. I hugged her and did my best to explain that I was canceling the wedding. Rosaura heard Chencha's bawling and came in my room to see what the fuss was about. She almost fainted from the news. She left and slammed the door. Chencha helped me get ready and I went downstairs to meet John.

With our hands held, we greeted our guests and told them that we were canceling our wedding as we returned their presents one by one. I don't know where I found the strength to handle the situation. It must have been from John. He stood beside me like an oak tree the entire time, except for an instant where he stepped aside to speak to Pedro. They spoke briefly and sealed their conversation with a firm handshake. John returned to my side and remained with me until all the guests were gone. No one stayed for the feast, so we asked Father Ignacio to distribute it to his congregation. Then John and I hugged good-bye, and we both cried plenty. I turned and rushed into the house so I didn't have to watch him leave. There will never be anyone else like John.

Dawn found the house completely silent this morning. The only sound is Chencha washing the dishes at the sink. I lay awake all night. I have a strange feeling of being in the wrong place, looking at the wrong things, hearing what I shouldn't. From my window I can see the empty chairs and bare tables that are waiting to be put away. I see dozens of vases piled in a corner, filled with flowers that are beginning to wilt. I look out upon a sunrise that should have found me at John's side. It's a timid, sad sun that is embarrassed to illuminate my sadness.

I have put away my wedding gown in a box. With this ritual I reclaim the title of "Miss Tita" and join the thousands of women who are alone due to death, impotence or indecision. I refuse to leave my room. I don't want to face anyone. I have no courage to do so. I haven't dared to unpack my clothing. These garments shouldn't be here, they should be at John's house, hanging in the grand wardrobe that was destined to be mine. John had it made especially for me, like the silver matchbox he slid into my palm before he left last night. It was his wedding present for me, one he didn't want to keep. Our names are etched on the inside. He made the matches himself and each one has a pyrographed letter that forms a poem I was to figure out like a puzzle. I feel like I will never be able to figure it out. If I can't find my own place in this world, how can I find this poem? How can I place each letter in its rightful place? There is nothing but indecision in my mind. I am afraid to become lost again, to become ill and not have my dear Dr. John Brown's hand nearby to save me. I received a farewell letter from him and reading it made me feel tremendously sad and alone. It's funny, just as I have such a profound physical connection with Pedro where I can't tell his hand from my own, with John I can't tell his thoughts from my own.

When I read his letter I immediately felt his deep pain and my eyes looked out upon an unknown landscape he must have been looking at. I can't make it out completely because tears blur my eyesight. But are they my tears, or are they John's?

Dear Tita,

I have not been able to sleep wondering who I am in your life. I think I am but a dream that disappears magically when it comes into contact with a reality that you and Pedro have built day by day. Tita, my dearest Tita, I need to go away for a time to mend myself, to try to find myself in another city, on another road, in another space. I can't do it here.

I am much too attracted to the idea of being the man who loves you and I must accept that I am not the only one who does. So I will go away for a time, because I feel out of place. I feel like I don't exist, that you conjure me when you say my name, when you call out to me, when you think of me. And I disappear when I bear witness to the beautiful, sad tenderness in your eyes when you look upon Pedro. For the time being I don't want to witness this anymore, and not out of jealousy, but because it's a masterpiece.

I need to remember who John Brown is without Tita by his side.

I need to achieve a state of peace and light so powerful that despite the distance I might reach you and envelop you in utter silence. I'll see you when I get there.

Forever yours, John.

This has been a complicated week. I have had seven days of goodbyes, arguments, gossip, changes, and crying, lots of crying. I don't think I have cried so much since the day I was born. I was told that I was born amidst a river of tears. Well, that might have been Nacha exaggerating but if that was true, I have cried a bigger river this past week. Esperanza helped me fill it. The poor girl has been crying constantly as well. Chencha told me she has refused to eat and does not want to be in Rosaura's bedroom. She only wants to be in the kitchen near the heat and the aromas that she has grown to love since she was born, but seeing as I have not come down to cook, Rosaura has kept the child by her side. I couldn't stand Esperanza's bawling anymore so I decided to break my voluntary confinement and came down to make lunch. I took Esperanza with me and Rosaura didn't complain in the slightest. Her eyes were also swollen from crying so much, probably due to Pedro's departure.

I had heard them arguing the previous nights and this morning he slipped a goodbye letter under my door. I read it and felt relief, knowing that I could leave my room without the danger of seeing him. I cooked a simple bean soup like Nacha used to make me, and added some rice and pieces of tortilla. Esperanza devoured it, stopped crying and fell asleep immediately. It was a relief for all of us. Making the most of the moment I took the child in my arms and headed to the room that used to belong to Nacha. It still smells of her. We lay in what used to be her bed and slept all afternoon. I'm sure Rosaura did the same because I heard no noise except for the cooing of my faithful pigeons who will never abandon me.

Tita,

I beg your forgiveness. I know that my behavior has been inexcusable and can only be explained as the product of my profound selfishness and my irrational jealousy, both of which are terrible counsel. Until this day I had not realized that those emotions clouded my mind and made me act in an indecorous and indecent manner. It wasn't until John talked to me that I understood the wrongness of my actions and I felt very ashamed. It was never my intention to hurt you, or Rosaura for that matter, but I was blinded by love and desire. And yes, I could only think of kissing you, touching you, holding you. I never thought of the consequences. And worst of all, I acted against my own self-interest.
You know well the motives that drove me to marry Rosaura. When you confronted me the other day I was hurt because I know life would have been better had I had the courage to steal you away, but I didn't want to place you in such a dishonorable position, or have people gossip about you. I didn't want you to be seen as an easy woman who would leave her house unmarried.
You know what they say about Gertrudis!

It wasn't until John opened my eyes that I realized that I was the one who devaluated your image in the eyes of others by making you my mistress, you whom I love more than anything in the world! You do not deserve this at all.
I'm writing this letter because I'm too ashamed to face you. If I could turn back time I would act differently. I promised John I would give you your rightful place. I have spoken to Rosaura and she refuses to divorce, so I have no choice but to leave the ranch. To have you near is torment. I need to put some space between us to protect you from myself. If you were able to give up such a great man as John, then I shall give you up as well, even if I die trying. That would be the greatest proof of my love. I will never touch or kiss you again, I don't need to do so to love you.

Yours truly,
Pedro Múzquiz

It seems almost impossible for me to lead a calm and organized life. No sooner were Rosaura and I agreeing on the best way to cohabit, when the house went topsy-turvy. I'm sorry, let me catch you up. I think I didn't even have the time to tell you that in order to allow Rosaura free reign over the house I moved into the dark room where I used to bathe mother, which later turned into the storage room in which I lost my virginity. It took me a while to clean, paint, repair and finally decorate the place. I love it because it's a small place that belongs only to me. In here I am the ruler, and I do as I please. I can put flowers wherever I want, knit whenever I want, I can read the chemistry books John gave me and even carry out small experiments here in a corner that I have fashioned into a tiny laboratory. I feel comfortable here. When I open my door it leads straight to the garden, and directly across it is the kitchen. The only times when I lose control over my space is when Esperanza comes in. She is a crawling whirlwind that wants to put everything in her mouth. I have to be very careful and watch her closely. Sometimes I prefer to let her out to the pens so she can play with the animals and become a bit distracted, but she really only wants to open all my drawers and play with my buttons and yarn. My room is a place of freedom for her, where I allow her to do as she pleases, unlike Rosaura who never lets her touch anything and slaps her hand at the slightest provocation. By the way, Rosaura is now giving piano lessons. I must say she is quite a good teacher. I like to hear her play, she has always been very talented. This makes me think that every cloud has a silver lining. Pedro's departure from the ranch has allowed Rosaura to do something she truly enjoys but never did before because she was dedicated to her domestic duties. Pedro tries to come every two weeks to bring money and visit

his family. I manage the ranch and cook while Rosaura teaches, which allows her to bring in a little extra money. We have reestablished some sort of family life.
To avoid temptation, when Pedro comes I stay in my room and don't come out until he leaves. I don't know what they do in the meantime. Look at me, I'm acting like Chencha, I start writing and I don't stop.
What I meant to tell you was that as soon as we were beginning to enjoy some peace and quiet, Gertrudis came back with her newborn son. She gave birth to a black boy last week and it was quite an uproar. Juan was furious because he thought my sister had been cheating on him and he offended her. And you know Gertrudis is a hothead! She took her child and left Juan. Fortunately I had kept all the correspondence between mother and Jose Treviño and I was able to clear things up. It was embarrassing to bring up mother's past like that but I was glad to be able to save my sister's honor.

Not that she really cared, but her marriage was at stake. Gertrudis was very grateful, but she still does not want to go back to Juan. She's very mad at him. Rosaura was so affected by it all that she fell ill. She suspended her piano lessons as a precaution because the gossip spread through the town like wildfire and she was afraid that mothers wouldn't let their children attend her classes.

Esperanza walking

Thank God, today Esperanza learned to walk. I say this because my back was close to breaking. She had been very restless for days, wanting to go to and fro, so I would lean down and hold her little hands so she wouldn't fall. Finally we resorted to tying one of Pedro's ties around her chest like a leash, and thus we were able to hold her while standing upright. When she took her first steps on her own I swept her up in my arms and ran to the house so we could show Rosaura. She enjoyed it so much! We both celebrated Esperanza's efforts and the child was so pleased with herself that she tried to clap and lost her balance and fell to the floor.

Esperanza has brought my sister and I closer. When she laughs, all is forgotten. We are no longer two sisters torn apart by the love of one man, but two sisters who share the love of a girl that gives us joy equally. You might say we are partners in Esperanza's upbringing. Alas, Gertrudis wasn't pleased about our celebrating.

She had not slept well because her baby son keeps her up at night. She was trying to nap while the child napped, and we woke her. I ran to get my photographic camera. John gave it to me as a present while I recovered at his house and he taught me to use it, but I hadn't had the opportunity to use it at the ranch yet. I took some photographs of Esperanza and ran to develop them in the small darkroom that John helped me set up. I tried to follow his instructions but it's harder to do so without him here to help. The photographs did not develop correctly, I think I chose an incorrect exposure, but at least I was able to capture the moment. I made one copy for myself and one for Rosaura, who was very grateful for it. Photography is just miraculous. I still don't understand how the process works, but it fills me with joy to show someone else what my own eyes saw, or to see on paper what someone else saw. It's exciting to know that Pedro will be able to see his daughter's

first steps even though he wasn't present.
While I was washing the photograph I thought of John and a story he told me of his grandmother. She would never let anyone take her photograph because she thought the camera could capture her soul. It made me think that if our spirit is light, then she is absolutely correct. Light definitely influences matter.

Corn that I have grown

Ash tanales or corundas

Cook black corn in ash water until it pops. Let it cool then wash well so the peel comes off easily. Then let it dry and add fresh cheese and ancho chiles that have been sitting in water with a pinch of salt. Grind all ingredients well. Wrap this dough in corn leaves and cook in a tamal cooker. When they are done let them cool and then fry them in oil before boiling them in a salsa made with tomato and green chiles.

Where there once was fire, ashes remain. I made these tamales in honor of mother today.

Dear diary,
guess what? We received an unexpected visitor today. Felipe Treviño, Gertrudis' half brother, came to the ranch. He's the son of Jose Treviño, the mulatto who was mother's lifelong secret love. Felipe showed up at our front door without warning and asked to see Gertrudis, but since she was napping, I offered to receive him. Rosaura didn't even want to see him. I led Felipe to the sitting room and he gave me a letter that his father gave him before passing. It was addressed "to the love of my life" and Felipe didn't know who this meant until Gertrudis' son was born. The poor man suffered greatly through our talk. He tried to be as polite as possible, as it was a very delicate subject. When he spoke his throat closed up and his voice quivered. I tried to make things easier on him by telling him that we were aware of the relationship between our mother and his father. Felipe was able to relax upon hearing this and

expressed his gratitude to us for helping him complete his mission. Felipe had sworn to his father on his deathbed that he would deliver this letter to the white woman with whom he had fallen in love and whose name he wasn't able to say before his final breath. Felipe never did anything to find out who the addressee was, but he didn't dare dispose of the letter either. He just kept it hidden from his mother. When the town erupted with rumors about Gertrudis' black child, Felipe felt obligated to give the letter to its rightful owner, my mother. When he found out mother was dead, he considered Gertrudis should have it, and wanted to meet her. It seemed that they were in fact, joined by blood. In my opinion this is clear. Although their skin tone is different, there is no doubt that they share the same father. Their eyes have the same shape, they share the same curly hair, thick lips and narrow nose, the product of the mixture of races.

When Felipe was about to take his leave, he heard Gertrudis' son cry and kindly asked to meet the boy. Felipe brought a knit sweater for the child, which seemed very thoughtful of him. I went upstairs and asked Gertrudis if the child could meet his uncle, and she said yes. Felipe looked at the child for a moment and kissed his forehead. He then said his goodbyes and paid his respects to Gertrudis. He left a card with his address in case my sister ever wants to meet with him. Rosaura was beside herself. She said that she did not approve of those people coming inside the house. Gertrudis, who has always been very direct, told Rosaura a thing or two and shut her up. I didn't even intervene in the argument, there was no reason to. I agree with Gertrudis that in order to end racism and slavery, civil wars and revolutions are necessary. And Gertrudis made it clear that "those people" are amongst the most valiant and brave that she had ever met, and to finalize she said that mother had seen no difference between Jose and father, because she had opened her legs for both of them. Rosaura almost fainted upon hearing this and locked herself in her room all night as a response to what she considered a great slight upon mother's memory. Gertrudis and I took this opportunity to read the letter José had written for mother and we both cried. It made me understand that one definitely can't judge a book by its cover. I now have a different image of mother and understand many things. What I still don't understand is why she tried to keep me from marrying if she knew from experience how unfair it was. I am grateful to Felipe for being brave enough to come to the house and giving me the opportunity to recreate in my mind a photograph of a woman who was willing to give up everything for love. Gertrudis is even more grateful than I. As soon as she finished reading the letter she asked me to look after her son and left to find Felipe. She later told me they spoke at length. Upon her return she began to pack her things because she intends to return to Juan tomorrow morning. She took the correspondence between mother and Jose as well as the locket with photographs of both of them that mother kept in her treasure box.

Dear Elena,

I write you this letter so you can learn the reasons that caused me to fail to meet you at the train station.

I know you walked from one end to another, searching for me, anxiously waiting and fearing I wouldn't be there on time. I know you held our Gertrudis with one arm and held Rosaura's small hand with the other. I know this because I was there, hidden, observing from afar. Fearful that your brothers might find me. Rafael saw me cross the bridge and was hot on my trail for a while, so I sought refuge at my aunt Julita's house. She asks why I don't give up on you, and fears for my life after your brothers' last attack. She thinks it unbelievable that your family persecutes me like I were a terrible murderer. I am surprised at this as well. We grew up together, for God's sake. When did my skin color become so offensive? Sometimes I wish I could hate them, but I can't. It was a blessing that my grandparents fled the Civil War in the United States to seek refuge in a place where their children wouldn't know slavery.

It was a blessing that your godfather gave them work and shelter for so many years, even though he was so attracted to my mother that he impregnated her when she was only 15 years old. If none of this had happened, I wouldn't be alive. I wouldn't be the mulatto that loves you madly. I would have never seen you, kissed you, loved you or impregnated you. I would have never known love.

If that was what I am to be condemned for, then I welcome it as a blessing as well. I am guilty and will gladly hang from a tree. If we had been allowed, you would be my woman now and we wouldn't have to hide from anyone. It breaks my heart to know that in my absence you had to return to your husband's house with your head hanging. This image hurts me more than the bullets they fired at me and the pain is greater than when they broke my bones. But let it be clear, I am not complaining. Everything I have suffered I would suffer again gladly if in the end I could have lived my last years in peace with you. I would risk anything for you. My safety, my life even, but during those hours that I watched you and waited I thought about Gertrudis and Rosaura. What right do I have to expose them to danger? What if we had indeed run away? Where could I have taken them that they would have been well received? A mulatto and a white woman are not well seen in society, period. That was why I chose to turn around and leave you, but I never turned my back on the love I have for you. Please raise Gertrudis as a free woman. May she never know slavery or prohibitions, let her lay on the grass and sunbathe whenever and wherever she may. Let her dance, laugh, gallop like mad, let nothing scare her from following her path, let her never have to choose between love or life. Teach her to see the world without prejudice. You never saw me as only your godfather's bastard, you saw me as something more than the color of my skin. You don't have to talk to our daughter about me, or about how she was conceived, her mere presence is a tribute to our love. And the moon will always be up in the sky, waiting for us.

José

It's incredible how fast time passes us by. It has now been two years since mother's death, since I cancelled my wedding to John, since Pedro left the house, since I moved into my new quarters. I thought I wouldn't survive so many farewells and changes and now I don't even have the time to sit and cry. I feel like a train track, run over by train after train without a rest, yet I must remain firm and unwavering. In this period of time Chencha gave birth to a beautiful girl she named Socorro. Gertrudis organized a wondeful baptism for her son Juanito here at the ranch and we hosted her entire troop before and after the event. Esperanza has befriended the sheep and they allow her to ride them. Rosaura's students now give small piano recitals. We have more cows now, and we sell cream and butter. My garden has grown considerably and in it I have planted new medicinal plants. At nights I still knit for a while before I fall asleep, exhausted from washing dishes, ironing diapers, putting mattresses out in the sun after the girls urinated on them, preparing porridge, watering plants... Sometimes I have the intention to write but I am too lazy to come up to the pigeon loft to fetch you, climb down down, write something and climb back up to hide you from Esperanza (the scribbles on previous pages are her work), and I forget about you. But today I was determined to update you on my culinary discoveries. It's what I told father Ignacio the day of Juanito's baptism, when he insisted that I could be damned for not going to church on a regular basis. I told him that didn't mean that I had strayed from God and reminded him that Saint Teresa said that God can be found even in stew. And I mean it. I can perceive a growing energy, a sort of spiritual essence that inhabits my pots and pans.

I don't know if I should call it God, or the masculine and feminine deities that Nacha fervently believed to inhabit the water, air, the seeds of corn, beans, or fire itself. To name it is irrelevant, but I definitely believe that a lot of important things happen when I cook. And I'm not talking about the mischief Esperanza and Socorro get up to when I am distracted at the stove, but about the changes made to the elements. Personal energy definitely influences food. I have been investigating this for some time now trying to find answers to all my questions. I'm always thinking about what we eat, where it comes from... what happens when food enters our body? And most of all, is light what really nourishes us? The book on chemistry that John gave me has no answers for this. All I have at my disposal is observation. I can see that sunlight is present in water. I have seen grandiose rainbows form when the sun comes out while it's raining and illuminates the water. Those water droplets can show us a color that was already there. I would like to be clear about this but it's difficult. According to the chemistry book, colors are light and vibration. The red of my tomatoes or the green of my peppermint are manifestations of light. So when I eat, I am eating light. If that light is vibration, a pulse, it is an energy current that transports information from one place to another. It's knowledge that comes from the skies. Sunlight, moonlight and starlight come into our mouths in the shape of color, aroma or flavor. Christmas rolls taste different if you let them stand in moonlight overnight, and sun dried meat has a different flavor as well.

Sometimes I think that if the absorption of light by organisms generates life, then we all eat light. You may wonder Dear Diary how I can affirm this if seeds grow into plants in the darkness. Well, a dark womb also creates life, but in both cases light is ever present as well. The clothing that future mothers wear affects the baby's gestation. It's inappropriate for an expectant mother to wear black, because the skin of a widow in mourning can even get stained because black is a color that

absorbs all light. It's important to notice that the light in the water they drink travels through their bloodstream.
The music they listen to can calm or alter the future baby. Let me tell you that the flowers that are nearest to the piano room where Rosaura gives her lessons grow better than the ones I plant anywhere else. They like to listen to music, which is also light. Light is always interacting with matter. It can be absorbed, reflected or transmitted. A tomato has light. An onion has light. Every product that the earth offers I can chop, fry, grind, or knead, but not so the light within them. That remains invisible and untouchable. The only thing that is certain is that I have discovered that love, like light, penetrates and transforms everything, and when I cook with love, people feel it. I have strived to feel that light and loving energy that the universe sends me. Can you imagine how many millions of years, of skies, of stars enter our bodies with

a simple gulp of water or a piece of tortilla? We eat the sky. We eat the earth. We eat air. We eat fire. We eat knowledge. I am moved almost to tears to think that the entire history of mankind enters through our mouth whenever we eat.

Esperanza among the peppermints

Health is a mystery to me. Sometimes it's more fragile than the wings of a butterfly. It can disappear from one moment to another and only once it's gone do we realize how much we need it and we seek help so that we can be well again. Fifteen days ago Esperanza contracted measles. She really scared us. She obviously gave it to Socorro, and I had to care for both girls as Chencha was pregnant once more and could not be exposed to contagion. Rosaura was not at the ranch. She had been invited to give a piano recital in San Antonio, Texas. Pedro had just left after his usual visit. I had to face the problem on my own. At first I didn't understand what was wrong with the girl. All I knew was that her malady couldn't be cured with chicken broth. It was a more complicated illness. We were sitting on the porch trying to feed the chickens and I thought it strange that Esperanza showed no signs of trying to run after them. She sat beside me and lay her

head in my lap. Her forehead was hot to the touch, and her eyes were red.
Her temperature was so high that it scared me. I took her upstairs to her room and put lard on the soles of her feet but it didn't help. The fever did not give way. Then I rubbed her feet with a mixture of water and rubbing alcohol and that cooled her down for a moment but then her temperature shot back up. Poor girl, she felt real bad and was crying a lot, so I decided to call John Brown. We had not seen each other since we cancelled our wedding. It was very difficult for me to pick up the telephone and ask the operator to connect me to him. I was afraid to hear his voice, but the urgent matter at hand meant that my fears and I had to step aside and not interfere. A woman answered and I froze. Who was she? It wasn't the voice of Caty, the cook. It sounded like a younger woman. I was besieged by jealousy. Had John married once again? I felt nauseous, but was

immediately embarrassed by my selfishness. I was the one who asked John to cancel the wedding, so I had no right to feel cross about him finding a new partner. Yet I always felt that he belonged to me completely. I tried to control myself and asked for Dr. Brown. The woman kindly informed me that he was with a patient but she would tell him I called as soon as he was finished. I felt like a fool giving that stranger my name and address. How to explain that I was once his betrothed? That John and I once loved each other so much that we were set to marry, that I wasn't a simple patient, that I was much more? I felt a lump in my throat. I made a great effort to answer that lady's questions about Esperanza's health and hung up as quickly as possible. The wait felt eternal, but it wasn't that long because as soon as John heard I had called and Esperanza was sick, he came running. In truth I never expected less, knowing John's ethical and moral commitment he has to all his patients as well as how much he cares for me. And then I thought I shouldn't be so sure about the last part, and that doubt plunged into my heart like the cold blade of a knife. The last time I had heard from him was about a year ago when he sent me a letter which revealed his feelings for me from his Aunt Mary's house in Pennsylvania.

Dear Tita,

I write this letter from my voluntary exile just to let you know that I am fine but I haven't found the peace I'm searching for. I'm not there yet. I need some more time before I come home. I don't want you to worry, it's just that internal change takes time. It must be assimilated and accommodated, and above all recognized. What I feel for you, Tita, is something I can't name. Call it constance if you will. It's ever present in my heart, and no one can take it away. It's not momentary. You don't even have to be close to me for me to feel it. This brings me to the acceptance of an idea I have had in my mind for a while: that time and space aren't real. Only light is real. You and I are not separate beings that live in different times and places, no. We once stared into each other's eyes, recognized each other and became one in the light. This is what I shall treasure. This is what keeps me alive. And I assure you, I'm happy. Don't feel sorry for me.

Eternally yours,
John Brown.

I ran to my room to find the letter
and read it several times before John
appeared at the front door with the hope
of returning Esperanza to health.
The letter couldn't have been clearer but
it had been a year and a half since he
wrote it and things might have changed.
Maybe that was why I felt so jealous to
see him arrive with Shirley, a beautiful
and quite affable nurse that came with
him. I assume it was the same woman who
took my call. There wasn't much time for
pleasantries. John introduced us briefly
and we immediately went to Esperanza.
Later John told me that Esperanza had
measles and since it's a viral disease
there was nothing to do but watch her
temperature so it doesn't rise too much.
He gave me a set of instructions and that
was all. I walked them out. Before we said
farewell I asked John about his carriage.
In a certain way I wanted to let Shirley
know that John and I had been friends
for some time now. It was childish of me

but I couldn't help it. John explained that he still kept his carriage but hardly used it anymore because his automobile allowed him to move faster and get to his patients sooner. As he spoke I looked at him intently. He was different. He had some gray at his temples that made him look more handsome and distinguished.
It stood out to me because he isn't old enough to go gray. His big blue eyes had a twinkle in them that I didn't know what to attribute to, maybe he was happy to see me, or maybe it was Shirley's companionship.
I wanted to tell him so much, to show him my small lab, talk about my experiments and listen to his advice, but it was a rushed doctor's visit and he left immediately. When John left I remained glued to the window, as though in a trance as I watched him drive away. Once the automobile was out of my sight I suffered an attack of jealousy and envy. Now I understand how Pedro must have felt when I was to marry John. It's incredible

how those ugly feelings can cloud a mind. Today I would have given anything to be the one riding next to John. That was my rightful place! I remembered that day long ago when when he rescued me from the pigeon loft and put me in his carriage. It was definitely a milestone in my life. Now I would give anything to go back in time and ride with him forever, with no set destination. Interrupted love, similar to disease, makes us value what we had before and pushes us to try to recover what we took for granted.

On second thought, what I just wrote is wrong. Jealousy, not love, is what's similar to a disease. A terrible one. I don't know how to cure it, but apparently John does. He is calm and at peace. I would say he is even content, despite our separation. It's obvious that his disease has successfully healed. And I don't think it was only due to time. No. There was something else. I wish he could tell me how to be at peace with seeing a loved one happy in the arms of another. How can one hide the pain that inevitably escapes the soul through one's gaze? I would like him to answer these questions and many more, but it wouldn't be correct. I must heal by myself, just like he did. There is no other way. I think for John it helped to put distance between us, and I can't do that. I would have to go very far away, to change my skin a thousand times until my body is the reflection of a mind that has defeated disease. Only then could I face John, proud of having healed instead of fearsome of showing the jealousy that corrodes me. I'm sure that he would notice the change immediately. He would notice that my gaze no longer screams for help, that I'm not about to break down in tears at any moment, that I have drunk from the celestial placenta that unites us completely, that I have discovered how to be in the light, in that paradise where everything changes and where everything that is lost can be found anew.

My cow and her calf

I've noticed that sometimes I have the false notion that everything is fine because I rise early, gather eggs milk the cows, feed my animals, grind corn for tortillas, get the bedpans from the bedrooms and wash them, I make breakfast, wash dishes, go to the market, begin cooking for dinner, I drop fruit peels and leftovers in my compost pile so that nothing goes to waste. Food always returns to food in a continuous cycle in which we all participate. In short, I accomplish all my tasks satisfactorily. Esperanza grows healthier, Rosaura not only does what she likes and has recovered her appetite, but is also losing weight. Chencha has enough milk to feed Socorro and her newborn son, who are only 10 months apart in age. Everyone is well. Everything is well. Everything grows. Everything blooms. We have everything we need and more, yet I can't shake the feeling that something's missing. It's not enough for me to fill my time with other people's needs to feel well

anymore. I feel like I let love slip by me. I failed to care for it, to prune it, to remove its dead leaves. I saw love come to life, grow and bear a beautiful fruit that I didn't look after so it could reproduce.
No, instead I let it fall to the ground and rot.
What a painful waste of life.

Rosaura has returned and is now caring for Esperanza. Pedro is home as well. When he learned his daughter was ill he came back earlier than he normally would. I imagine that after Roberto's death he is terrified that Esperanza might contract a deadly disease.
It has been a relief for me that they are here, that way I don't have to see John and Shirley when they make their visits. The girl is recovering and is much better, which I am thankful for.
Rosaura has been very kind to me these past few days. If anyone understands jealousy it's her, and she has been very understanding towards me. I am very moved by her attempts to tell me about John without me asking her to. She has informed me that John and Shirley are not romantically involved, she is only his trainee. I don't know if Rosaura is playing matchmaker out of the kindness of her heart, or if she only intends for me to get back together with John so she can be

rid of me. Maybe I am being unfair and she really does care about my happiness. I am grateful for her efforts and to be honest I was quite relieved to know that John and Shirley are not romantically involved. But it's only a partial relief, because that isn't the real problem.

I am the problem. My selfishness scares me. I have a desire to be special in someone's life, be it Pedro, John, even Esperanza.

I think it's necessary that I open my heart. Maybe tonight I'll prepare myself a cup of hot chocolate.

Hot Chocolate with chile and achiote

Ingredients:

1 kilogram cacao (preferibly Soconusco)

1 kilogram sugar

30 grams achiote

1 toasted arbol chile

Instructions:

Toast the cacao beans and grind them in the metate like in the previous chocolate recipe. The only difference is that when grinding, you should add the achiote and toasted arbol chile. When the paste is uniform, shape the tablets with your hands and mark them with the tip of a knife before laying them out to dry. If the chocolate will be drunk as part of a ritual ceremony, do not add sugar. It's also not advised to mix it in milk, use water instead. If it's too bitter, you may add a teaspoon of agave syrup.

Last night before bed I made myself a cup of hot chocolate and sipped it slowly as part of a ritual I have been imagining, recreating, or inventing, whatever you may call it. From the moment I began the preparations I could clearly hear Nacha's voice suggesting I add a bit of achiote and chile. I obeyed. I never questioned her commands in the kitchen while she was alive, I wasn't going to start now.
She is a great shaman. When I drank the chocolate I entered a strange state. In spite of having my eyes closed, I could see lights of all colors that became luminous presences. Don't ask for explanations as to why I saw what I saw, just believe that before my eyes appeared the faces of Nacha and Morning Light, who began to chant to me in their native tongues and my heart began to beat to the rhythm of their song. The strength of the beat increased until I felt my heart explode into millions of small pieces and within it a light emerged

that yanked me forcefully out of my body and shot me straight into the heart of the Milky Way. The only thing that kept me tethered to earth was a single silver thread. It was isolated, loose and fragile. For a moment I felt lost and thought that my thread would snap loose. Then Nacha and Morning Light took my thread and began to knit it with other threads that were just as luminous, which I recognized as belonging to mother and my sisters. It was comforting to feel that my thread formed part of a beautiful fabric that transformed, changed and became stronger. I understood that an isolated thread can't resist on its own, it comes unraveled. On the other hand, a knitted thread acquires the strength of thousands. I felt at home. And as if I were Alice in Wonderland or any other character in a fantasy tale, every time my thread joined that of another human I could see their faces light up like the fluorescent lamps Tesla invented that so marveled John when he saw them at the Chicago World's fair. But as usual, I digress. What I really wanted to tell you is that every face I saw had bright blue eyes, an electric blue that is hard for me to explain. I stared at mother's face for a while and saw that we are very alike in appearance. You could say we were the same person, staring into a mirror. We looked into each other's eyes for a moment and I noticed that from her pupils and mine emerged light currents like umbilical cords, and they allowed us to feed one another. Her eyes seemed to tell me that she knew what I know. Our eyes welled up with tears, and we hugged. I understood that the strands that join me to everything and everyone are unbreakable. No one is ever truly alone. I saw that Shirley is just me with another face, that it doesn't matter who John is closest to. We are all part of the same fabric, of a great, loving bedspread. The love I felt was so strong that I blessed Shirley for being close to John and giving him the company that I could not. I understood that love is not about bodies. It flows freely within us at all times. It is an energy that lovingly takes our individual threads and knits them into this huge, luminous blanket. Last night I cried from so much love. But it was a type of love that I had never known, a never-ending love that cannot go to waste, that doesn't evaporate or die, that always remains.

I am eternally grateful to the Chocolate for the gift it gave me.

I tried to draw a cacao tree.

Esperanza wrote the title.

arbol de cacao

Mama

This morning I arranged an altar for Nacha and Morning Light. I decorated it like a Day of the Dead altar.
It's quite pretty. The only difference is that since it's not marigold season, I used some beautiful flowers from my garden instead. Everything else adhered to tradition. All four elements were represented properly: fire by candles, air by incense, earth by flowers and instead of water I placed a gourd with some foamy hot chocolate. Thank God I still had some chocolate bars left over that Chencha brought back from her town in Oaxaca. I took special care in preparing the chocolate. I was very careful to wait until the water was about to boil before adding the tablet and then I kept the water from coming to a boil.
As soon as it foamed I removed it from the fire. I let it stand for a few minutes then put it on the fire again. I repeated this three times before I whipped the chocolate. It was the best way to honor Nacha and Morning Light, to thank them

for being by my side during my chocolate ceremony. Esperanza stood beside me for the entire time it took me to prepare it. She had been brought to the kitchen because she'd gotten restless and tired of being in her room. Her recovery has been impressive. The measles are a thing of the past. The clearest proof of this is that she began to chatter wildly again, asking about everything she could. I patiently answered all of her questions. I told her that these altars are set up on special occasions but especially on Day of the Dead so the people who have left this world can return and enjoy the meals we prepare for them. Esperanza asked me if this altar was for the woman whose photograph we placed at its center. I said yes, that was Nacha, and she asked if Nacha was my mother. No, I answered, but I loved her like a mother and that is why I'm making chocolate for her, I'm sure she will like the smell of it. And how will she smell her chocolate if she is dead, Tita? That was when things got complicated. It's not easy to explain matters of the spirit to a three-year old girl. I myself would like for someone to answer that and many other questions I have. It would be a relief for someone to assure me that I will be able to look after and care for Esperanza from the afterlife and that she will be able to see and hear me like I can see and hear Nacha. That she will be able to look to me for help when she is grief-stricken. That she will forever feel the profound love I have for her. It's hard for me to accept that some day I will have to leave Esperanza and won't bear witness to her joy or sorrow. I will no longer hear her chattering, her laughter, or her singing. It's hard for me to think about death. And as if she could hear my thoughts, the girl then asked: when you are dead, who will make an altar for you if you don't have children of your own? Well, anyone who remembers me can make one, I said. And she answered: I will always remember you. Well, then you must pay attention and learn to make the chocolate so you can make it for me one day, I answered as we laughed. I thought that was the end of that, and we left the kitchen to feed the chickens. It wasn't until later when I returned to my room that I found you open on my bed, Dear Diary, and saw that Esperanza had written the word "mom" on you. When did she learn how to write? It's a complete mystery. She had been asking me about letters for the past few days. She would take one of my books, point to a letter with her tiny finger and ask: how do you say this? I never thought she would figure out how to join letters to make a word, much less write it.

Dill Pickles

20 dill cucumbers
½ teaspoon powdered alum
1 clove garlic
2 heads dill
1 red hot pepper (if wanted)
1 quart vinegar
3 quarts water
1 cup salt

Wash cucumbers, let stand on ice water one night. Pack in sterile jars.
To each quart, add alum, garlic, dill.
Combine vinegar, salt and water, and bring to boil. Fill jars. Place dill in bottom.

Today was a day of great contrast.
Since my experience with the chocolate I have enjoyed several days of calm.
My mood had been joyful and content, but today Gertrudis exasperated me.
I was making some pickles for John as a thank you for his help with Esperanza.
He tended to her with great care and tenderness and he refused to accept payment for his services. Rosaura and Pedro asked me to cook something for him and I thought I would make pickles like Caty had taught me. It's a recipe that has been in John's family for some time now.
As it's not a recipe I'm accustomed to, it required my complete attention in every step. So there I was, concentrated, when Gertrudis called on the telephone.
Don't take this the wrong way, because it scares me to be like Rosaura who is afraid of everything that even smells of change, but I really dislike talking with the receiver against my ear! I'm not opposed to modernity, but I am still

not completely convinced it is the best thing to have a telephone in the house. I understand that we were blessed to have it when Esperanza fell ill. But suddenly people feel like one is only sitting around the house waiting for the apparatus to ring and have a chat, when that's not the case. Not for me, at least. I have many tasks to attend to, I can't just sit around doing nothing. The ringing of the telephone breaks my concentration, and conversations that go on too long are even worse. I can't cook in peace.

The worst part was that I couldn't find a way to end the conversation with Gertrudis today, because she was quite cross, and with good reason. She told me that the newly drafted Mexican Constitution chose to not give us women the right to vote under the argument that women don't feel a need to participate in public affairs, as proven by the lack of collective moments in that regard! Can you imagine how insulting this is to someone who actively participated in the Revolution, who risked her life and was a firsthand witness of the role that women soldiers played in the struggle? Well, Gertrudis was enraged. I let her vent until she cooled down a bit and when we hung up the vinegar for my pickles was frothing, a clear sign that it was spoiled and I had to start again. I know it's not a big deal, certainly not as comparable to the thought that we need another revolution in order to draft a new Constitution that will do justice to women. The only thing that gave me comfort was knowing that my decision to stay at home to try to change things in my family cannot be considered a failure yet. We shall see.

Gertrudis' friends.

Esperanza hasn't shut her mouth since she learned to talk. She can be overwhelming. You know how I enjoy her quirks but lately she has been getting in too much trouble on account of her curiosity.
She chose this day to attack me with a barrage of questions while we wrapped our Christmas presents. The red of the bows detonated her thirst for knowledge and she asked why I placed red-tinted paper on the windows when she had the measles. "Because my mother did the same thing when I had the measles," I answered. And she just kept going. "Why do chickens lay eggs? Why is Gertrudis' baby black? Why don't you have a gentleman caller? Why doesn't Daddy live at home? Why must I eat vegetables? Why do two dogs sometimes get stuck together and can't separate?" I answered all of her questions, trying to remain as superficial as possible. The hardest question was about her cousin Juanito's skin color. I answered that Juanito was black because his grandfather

was black too. Oh! she replied. If I had known such a simple answer would have been enough, I wouldn't have fretted so much about finding answers appropriate for her age. I thought that had been the end of it, but she insisted later.

"But Tita, what about the dogs?"

Fortunately Socorro came along to ask her to play and she forgot about everything. I was saved by the bell. But then I got to thinking about my answers and realized one never knows exactly why we do what we do. We might call this force of habit. We repeat actions without thinking about it, and that becomes tradition. I truly don't know why red-tinted paper is placed on windows when someone is ill with the measles, nor why lately we decorate a tree for christmas instead of setting up the nativity scene, nor who decided Christmas rolls should become an institutional part of Christmas dinner, nor why this family has this cursed tradition of lonely women.

Last night we celebrated Christmas Eve. Rosaura invited John and Alex to dine with us. I think it was in part a show of gratitude, but also a scheme to bring John and me back together. I'm grateful either way. It was a very pleasant evening.
At first I felt a certain tension between Alex and I because of the cancelled wedding. I felt that he looked at me reproachfully. He didn't play with me like we used to, but it was completely understandable. Fortunately Esperanza's presence lightened the mood. They got along wonderfully despite their age difference. Alex is about to turn eight and Esperanza is three. When it came time to open the presents Esperanza hugged Alex and kissed his cheek. The boy seemed intimidated but I could tell he enjoyed the show of affection as well. Rosaura was not happy about that at all. She discreetly took her daughter by the hand to a corner away from everyone and told her that she cannot go around kissing boys. Obviously Esperanza asked why, and I wasn't able to hear my

sister's answer. Fortunately I don't think the warning scared her because later on I saw her kiss Alex's cheeks again, away from her mother's prying eyes. The biggest success was our choice of presents for the children. John gave Esperanza a small microscope to satisfy her thirst for knowledge and she loved it! I fetched an onion peel from the kitchen and helped Esperanza set up her present to observe it. She marveled at the colors and textures she could observe.
Alex was also very pleased with the roller skates we gave him, and he immediately tried them out in the living room, much to Rosaura's distress. My best present was the ability to hug John, if even for a moment. It filled me with peace, and honestly, so did the fact that Shirley didn't come.
But what I enjoyed the most was when Alex and I shared a hug like we used to. It was a sincere and open show of affection. I feel like the heat that emanated from my heart when I held him in my arms was warm enough to melt the layer of ice that had

stood between us, and this lifted my spirits. I love when things transform. Ice becomes water that flows, that cleans, that moistens eyes. Fortunately in this case the layer of ice wasn't too thick, otherwise it would have taken longer to melt it. The larger and denser the matter, the longer it takes to transform it. A big chunk of ice like the one in my ice box takes much longer to melt than a lemon sorbet.

Miss
Josefina De la Garza
Hidalgo 709-
P. Negras, Coah.

Made in France - Fabriqué en France

Merry Christmas Tita!
We wish you the best
for the New Year.
Gertrudis, Juanito
and Juan.

December 1st, 1916

One doesn't notice illness until it's too late, when it's already manifested, when there's nothing to do about it. It develops slowly and invisibly inside of us without warning. If one could learn in advance of the plotting of bacteria against our cells, it would be different story.

One month and a half ago I fell ill to typhoid fever. It was grave, I was bedridden for a month. My strength is only now returning and the first thing I want to do is write about my experience.

It all began on a day when I felt a cold coming on. My head hurt and my body ached. I lay in bed and fell asleep, but was soon awakened by a sharp pain in my midsection and a general malaise.

My body was shaking with cold. I threw on a blanket and it didn't help. Soon my temperature began to rise and nothing could control it. Chencha was alarmed so she fetched Rosaura, who then telephoned John but couldn't reach him. His Aunt Mary had passed away and he had traveled to Pennsylvania for the funeral. Fortunately Shirley was there to take the call and she kindly offered to come visit me. I felt so terrible that I didn't object. I must admit that I owe my life to her. She quickly diagnosed me correctly and administered medication. She would visit me every day, something I looked forward to. She has a wondeful bedside manner. I don't know if it was due to my high fevers, but on some days I could see Nacha and Morning Light beside her. Whenever she put a wet cloth on my forehead I swear I could feel Nacha's hands acting through Shirley. Of course I did not tell this to anyone. I don't want anyone to make light of something so serious. But the most amazing thing happened during one of her visits when Shirley brought Alex along because there was no one else to watch him. Alex and Esperanza ran around the patio, I could hear them hollering and giggling. Alex took Esperanza by her braid and yanked, and my niece was

so upset that she said "I'm gonna tell your grandma on you."
Alex laughed and said: "My grandma's dead." "What?" said Esperanza,
"Your grandma's right here! I can see her, she came to look after my Tita and she says she will tug on your feet at night if you're not good to me." Alex was at a loss for words. What Esperanza said confirmed that I'm not mad, that others can also see presences like I can. What is it that allows some of us to see, but not others?
Does it come naturally children?
Why does it only happen to me under specific circumstances? I don't know. What I do know is that I saw Nacha and Morning Light assisting Shirley. That's a fact.
But it doesn't mean that I'm not eternally grateful to Shirley for her devoted care. I don't know how I can ever thank her. Never in my 21 years of age had I felt so bad. Every day she would arrive early in the morning to see how I had slept. She helped Chencha change my sweat-soaked bedsheets

and even offered to take them home to wash
and iron because Chencha could barely
handle the workload here at home.
It was a good thing too, because she would
iron my sheets with lavender water and
I'll never forget the wonderful sensation of
crawling into a bed with perfectly ironed
and perfumed sheets. I'm sure that influenced
my recovery. Shirley's help was instrumental.
I'm grateful that it was her and not John
who nursed me back to health. John would
have made me feel intimidated, whereas
Shirley didn't. I felt very at ease with her.
I was so weak that Shirley and Chencha had
to hold me in their arms to give me a sponge
bath and change my nightgown. Later, when
Chencha took my dirty clothes and bedpan,
Shirley cleaned my scalp with a towel and
orange blossom water. She then brushed
and braided my hair, and held a bucket
so I could clean my teeth, and didn't leave
until I was clean and fresh. Her care was
a true blessing. Shirley will never know this,
but she not only nursed me back to health

physically, she also removed invisible wounds that can only be healed with love. There is no medicine, pill or ointment that can cure jealousy, only love can. Since my disease I no longer consider Shirley a rival, but a sister. If she marries John I will understand and accept it gladly.
John deserves someone like her in his life.

Dear Diary,

you must think I'm shameless. Again I let almost two years go by without writing in you. Time flies and there's no stopping it. I think it's important to mention that John and Shirley finally married. It didn't come as a surprise, it was something I saw coming from the beginning but it took time for them to recognize how they felt about each other and to begin a romantic relationship. Three months before the ceremony, John, gentleman that he is, came to see me and was attentive enough to tell me that he had decided to marry Shirley. He wanted me to be the first to know. I had nothing but praise for Shirley and congratulated him profusely on his decision. Don't think it was an effort for me. I truly spoke my mind. I won't deny that I felt a small pang in my stomach upon hearing the news but it was nothing compared to the first time I saw them together. That jealousy has been left behind. Our conversation was

brief because we were both very emotional, despite our only remaining link being one of pure friendship. We hugged for a long time after we talked. It may seem strange that I can write this so calmly but this is how I feel. I think it's the best thing for John and Alex. My 22 years of age have made me mature and accept things that a few years ago I wouldn't have had the capacity to face. I think that this is in part due to the respect and gratitude I have for Shirley. She will be the best mother and wife in the world, this I know.
We all went to the wedding.
Esperanza carried the train of Shirley's gown and they both looked gorgeous. like two princesses. Before entering the church, Shirley took me aside and thanked me for attending. I said that I was honored to be there and reminded her that I could be present only because she saved my life. We embraced like sisters.
In general, the word I can use to describe the wedding is joyful. It was a joyful

wedding. Happiness was present at all times, from the moment the bride and groom entered the church, until the very end. During the reception Esperanza danced and danced. On her own mostly, but she dragged Alex to the dance floor when she could although he ran away just as quickly. Alex is now 10 years old and is embarrassed to dance in public, but Esperanza has no such fear. I so enjoy seeing her happy because I feel that when Esperanza laughs the stars can see their reflection in her eyes. She danced and danced and didn't stop until it was time for the bride and groom to cut the cake. I baked the cake at Shirley's request. Modesty aside I must admit that it was delicious and after eating it I was invaded by a feeling of euphoria so strong that I disregarded all etiquette manuals and danced Charleston with Esperanza! I was exhausted after 5 songs and had to step outside to the garden for fresh air. It smelled of night-blooming jasmine, one of my favorite flowers. From the bench where I sat I could see that everyone was enjoying the party. By then Esperanza had abandoned the dance floor and was catching fireflies with Alex, who had more experience in the matter. Esperanza was yelling and running wildly. I don't know where she got the energy, or where all the fireflies came from. When she had caught a couple she put them down the front of her dress and they shone through the fabric. It was very amusing and Alex laughed a lot. I shall never forget that night filled with fireflies, night-blooming jasmine, joy and love.

Today was Esperanza and Socorro's first communion. They looked stunning in the white dresses I designed and made for them. I used the fabric of the wedding gown I would have worn had I married John. It was just enough for the two dresses. I was able to finish them in time because I used my new Singer sewing machine. Mother would have never believed me! She always refused to get one. She didn't like sewing in the midst of such a "racket." She considered sewing afternoons the best time for communication and relaxation. I agree with the sentiment, except she never allowed my sisters and I to choose the subject of conversation. She was always repressive. Yet again, I digress. The point is I was able to sew the frilled dresses in only one week. Chencha and I decided to make Norteño Tamales for breakfast and I don't think it was the best idea. They were delicious, but since Chencha invited all her relatives we had to make hundreds of tamales, and I get tired more easily at my age. I don't have the same energy I used to have. But it was worth it. The mass was beautiful. Patricia, Paquita Lobo's niece, played the organ. She is a student of Rosaura's, so my sister had a double reason to cry during the ceremony. I noticed that Felipe never took his eyes off of Patricia. I think he is too young to be noticing girls, but true to Gertrudis' spirit he is very precocious. Alex isn't lagging behind on that subject either. He is now 14 and it's logical for him to be attracted to girls, but I think Esperanza, being only 9, is much too young for him. Yet in matters of the heart nothing is set in stone. I saw how Alex looked at Esperanza as she walked down the aisle. His eyes were sparkling. Pedro noticed this as well and looked at me with complicity. We shared a smile. Fortunately Rosaura was so busy drying her tears that she didn't notice.

Norteño Tamales

Ingredients:

1 ½ kgs. tamal dough
½ kg. lard
½ kg. fatty pork meat (head, loin, etc)
100 grams ancho chile
Garlic, cumin (freshly ground), onions and salt
Corn husks for wrapping

Instructions:

Cook the meat with the garlic, onion and salt. Once cooked remove from the broth, shred and chop. Keep the broth.
Chiles must be de-veined and cooked in water. Grind them along with cumin and salt. This salsa must be fried with a bit of lard and boiled for a moment.
Later, add the chopped meat and a little bit of the broth, so that it is not too dry nor too soppy.
Whip the lard with your fist until it rises, then add the tamal dough and knead.

It's convenient to add a little bit of the broth with chile to give it color, as well as some of the broth that was set aside. Continue whipping until it rises more and there are no more lumps. To know if it has been whipped enough, take a pinch of it and drop it in a glass of water. If it floats, it's ready. Before the tamales are made, taste the dough to see if it's not missing salt.
Set the corn husks soak in warm water and cut their tips so they are all the same size. Add some dough to each husk and place the meat in the center. Roll and fold the husk. These tamales must be placed in the tamal cooker filled with water. Place tamales so that the folded side is facing down. Finally add a bed of husks on top and a rag. Cook at high fire for an hour and a half. To check for readiness, remove a tamal and open it. If the husk does not stick to the dough, they are ready.

Dear Diary,
I appreciate having you in my life, but it wasn't necessary for you to drop straight on my head! I understand that if you hadn't dove from the top of my dresser where I put you so long ago you might still be sitting there, but it truly hurt.
I have so much to tell you, that I don't even know where to begin. Yesterday we went to a birthday party for Annie, Shirley and John's daughter. She is already 6 years old! Yes, almost the same amount of years that I have abandoned you. Annie is gorgeous, and she can already read. Can you believe it? She's well loved and cared for. Shirley made hot-dogs for the kids who came to the party. She makes the sausages following a recipe she learned from her German grandmother. I helped Shirley grind the meat in my meat grinder and they turned out delicious. The tomato sauce was just as good, we made it using tomatoes from my garden. It's surprising how quickly

this meal has become a favorite amongst children. According to John, it was also at the Chicago World's Fair where a man with a street cart decided to sell a frankfurter inside a bun and called it a hot-dog. Rosaura thinks this is a highly offensive name, but I find it amusing. It was surprising that Rosaura accepted to come to the party at all. Under any other circumstance she would have refused, because since Esperanza turned 12 she tries at all costs not to let her come into contact with Alex. But since Annie is one of her favorite piano students, she agreed to come. I guess Esperanza must have been under a stern warning because she remained glued to her mother throughout the party. When the hot dogs were ready everyone approached the grill and I took this as an opportunity to step inside the house. I love the smell of medicine that comes from its walls. It always comforts me and takes me back to when I recovered in those very rooms. I was strolling down memory lane when I heard Rosaura yelling and Esperanza sobbing. I ran to the yard and encountered my sister making a terrible scene. Apparently Esperanza and Alexhad been eating their hot-dogs next to each other when Esperanza spilled some tomato sauce on her dress. Alex, trying to help her, quickly used a damp napkin to wipe the sauce off her dress. Unfortunately the sauce had fallen on her chest. I would have done the same, because if one doesn't act immediately then the sauce can leave a permanent stain, but according to Rosaura, Alex was only using this as an excuse to touch my niece's breasts. She loudly and publicly accused him of being a corrupter of minors because any decent seventeen-year old boy should know perfectly well not to touch a young girl's chest. It was highly embarrassing for everyone. We were forced to leave the party amidst Esperanza's sobs and everyone's bewilderment.

Frankfurters

3 feet sheep or small (1-½ inch diameter) hog casings
1 pound lean pork, cubed
¾ pound pork fat, cubed
¼ cup very finely minced onion
1 small clove garlic, finely chopped
1 teaspoon sweet paprika
1 teaspoon freshly fine ground white pepper
1 teaspoon cinnamon
1 egg white
1 teaspoon sugar
1 teaspoon salt, or to taste
¼ cup milk

Soak the casings in cold water for half an hour, then wash thoroughly. After that, soak them in vinegar water to soften, while you prepare the meat filling.

Grind the beef, pork and pork fat. Then mix the rest of the ingredients and grind finely. Finally, mix all the ingredients with meat, egg white and milk.
With this mixture, stuff the casings.

Yesterday my sister Rosaura passed away. It came as a complete surprise to everyone. For several days she had been suffering from a terrible indigestion, which caused her to have excessive gas. She even complained of heart palpitations but John told her it was probably due to the same intestinal inflammation that was creating pressure on her heart. I immediately felt responsible for her death because I had been so angry at her for the past week that I surely transferred some of that uncontrollable evil energy to the food while I cooked and that affected her so much that it killed her. Although it was strange that no one else seemed affected by what what I cooked, and we all ate the same food. The only other person who complained of appetite related problems was Esperanza, but that must have been due to how upset her mother was making her. Rosaura had forbade her from ever seeing Alex again. He had been courting her for months and Rosaura had

always been opposed. Esperanza cried, protested and begged for my sister's understanding but Rosaura's position was firm: Esperanza was not allowed to have a "boyfriend", much less marry. Period. Esperanza turned to Pedro for support but he wasn't much help. The only thing he achieved was for Rosaura to stop talking to him. I tried to intercede on Esperanza's behalf and only got the same result. Even Shirley tried to reason with Rosaura but my sister refused to listen and asked that she kindly mind her own business.
She refused to budge. Nevertheless, her death now gives Esperanza and Alex an open path to love. From an outsider's perspective this may have seemed like a planned murder with myself as the main suspect. I would agree, in fact, I declare myself guilty. It has been a while now since I have proven that energy influences food. I should have let Chencha do the cooking, or made other

arrangements. Fortunately John and Shirley arrived very soon after Rosaura passed away and after examining the body John told us that the cause of death was a heart infarction. Upon hearing this, I sighed with relief. I still have my doubts, but if I intend to live the rest of my life free of guilt, I must believe John. Esperanza cried throughout the entire funeral. When I approached her to comfort her she confessed that she felt very guilty. I asked her why, and she said that she felt responsible for her mother's death. She told me that the previous night Rosaura had caught her and Alex kissing on the front porch of the house and had gone mad. Rosaura yelled at Alex to leave her property and yanked Esperanza up to her room. Immediately afterwards my sister, still fuming, had locked herself in her room. Esperanza assumed this incident had brought on her heart failure. It wasn't until I heard my niece say this that I realized how we believe we have more power over others than we really do, and that is an act of arrogance. Yes, our actions may affect others, but there's a long way between that and indirectly causing their death. I decided not to tell her that I had considered myself responsible for Rosaura's death, and instead decided to confess that many times I had wished death upon my mother because I wanted to marry and she forbade it. I told Esperanza that it took me years to finally understand that my wishes didn't cause mother's death. It was her own guilt that did it. She feared that I was trying to kill her as an act of vengeance, and that drove her to drink too much Ipecac syrup as an antidote. She caused her own death. As I talked, my mind acquired a great clarity. My initial intention was only to comfort Esperanza but in the end I healed along with her. I told Esperanza that if she didn't cast away the guilt from her mind, sooner or later it would turn against her, because believing she had caused her mother's death automatically made her the guilty party. In the eyes of society every guilty person deserves punishment, so if no one else punished her she would seek to punish herself. And what better punishment is there than to think one does not deserve to give and receive love? That's not the fate she deserves. She has every right to love and be loved.

Finally, I told her that maybe her mother did indeed want her to be happy, but the only way she knew how to allow that was by stepping aside. We hugged for a long time as our hearts and thoughts healed.

It's funny how history repeats itself. It seems there are certain dates and sequences that come full circle and have influence over us, whether we are conscious of it or not. It's like day and night. Like the sowing and reaping seasons, like the time for activity and the time for rest. Today we received Alex and his parents when they came to ask for Esperanza's hand in marriage, and there we were, in the same spot where Pedro and Don Pascual once came to ask for my hand in marriage, and where years later, under other circumstances, John did the same. Certain places are destined for encounters, for the crossing of roads. The sitting room hasn't changed one bit. The sofas have the same upholstery, the paintings still hang in their same place on the walls. The only touch of modernity is given by a shiny radio that makes our phonograph look positively ancient. Yet, the protagonists of the story are still the same. The cast has hardly changed. The only one absent is Rosaura. Well, Shirley is also a late addition to this company, but other than her the rest of us have been playing these roles for years with as much dignity one can muster when partaking in tales of forbidden love. But I'm filled with joy to know that there is a possibility for a new ending, one in which the loving couple will be allowed to marry the person they choose. That is certainly cause for celebration!

I cooked the chicken breasts in asparagus sauce that Esperanza loves, and I set the table as beautifully as I could. I filled the house with flowers and candles and at the end of the night I raised my glass and toasted the happy couple.

Chicken Breasts in asparagus sauce

3 chicken breasts, halved

150 grs. cream

3 tablespoons mayonnaise

550 gr. preserved green asparagus

juice from two limes

2 teaspoons salt

2 garlic cloves

½ onion

small stalk of cilantro

1 can of morron chile, cut in strips

Instructions:

Cook chicken with onion, garlic, cilantro and 1 teaspoon salt. Once they are done let them cool in the ice-box for one day and then filet them.

Mix cream, mayonnaise, asparagus, lemon juice and a teaspoon of salt to taste in blender. Then sift this sauce.

On the platter where you will serve this dish, make a bed of the sauce, then place a layer of the breast filet, and repeat.

Garnish with the asparagus tips and moron chile strips to make it look like poinsettia flowers. Serve cold. As a side you can serve asparagus that have been sautéed with a little salt.

Yesterday I awoke feeling a pit in my stomach, dreading to exit my bedroom. It was the first time in many years that Pedro and I were together with no other family member around. With no one to see us, no one to repress us, no one to judge us except, of course, ourselves. Pedro and I have both spent our lives hiding our feelings for each other.

For many years we have glanced at one another without really looking. We hear the other without listening, brush against each other without touching, speak without saying anything. It was hard for me to become accustomed to dealing with a cold and distant man. The coldness Pedro imposed on our relationship was such that it burned me, like dry ice. Not even when I was close to dying from typhoid fever was Pedro able to lift the formality he had imposed on himself.

He brought me flowers and visited frequently but kept his distance. Maybe in order to keep a proper in-laws

relationship it was necessary that he
tie himself up in a corset of etiquette
rules that kept him rigid, tight and
constrained. But just like any tie sooner
or later must come loose, Pedro finally
burst from so much pressure, and it
happened yesterday.
Esperanza left for the capital to find the
lace she wanted for her wedding dress.
Shirley traveled with her because since
Chencha asked me to be godmother to her
granddaughter, Socorro's girl, I had to
stay home. The party will take place in
a couple of days so all the workers are
very occupied with organizing the baptism.
There is still much to do. A great number
of sheep and chickens must be slaughtered
so we can make mole and barbecue for
all of Chencha's relatives. I rose early
and bathed so I could go downtown to
fetch the gold medallion I had engraved
with the girl's name (by the way I don't
understand why she is to be named after
her grandmother, but that was Socorro's

decision and the girl shall be named Crecencia). I just hope she doesn't wind up with the nick-name "Chenchita" to tell her apart from Chencha. Anyway, as I was getting dressed to go get the medallion I saw Pedro from my window, who was out picking flowers. When I came down for breakfast I noticed he had placed them in a vase in front of Rosaura's photograph, along with a candle. Then he went for a ride on his bicycle. A few minutes later I heard him return. He had fallen and his arm was scraped up badly. When he was washing up at the sink I approached him with the intention to help. He turned his face so I couldn't see his tears. I put a hand on his back and he shook it off violently. "Don't come near me!" he yelled. Then, with a hoarse voice that I had never heard before, he said "can't you see that I can't take this any more? That I'm tired of failing? I tried to love Rosaura, but I couldn't. I have tried to respect your sister's memory..." I cut him off, saying

"and so you have." This upset him even further and and his voice turned even more heartbreaking as he said "You know nothing Tita! I never should have loved you!, I never should have married your sister, in fact I wish I was never born, at least I would have spared you all from the harm I've inflicted!" I asked him to lower his voice and he answered "Do you really not see?" "What?" I asked.
He paused and said "That I love you madly and I can't respect you any longer." He then led me by the hand to my bedroom. Fortunately Chencha and the workers were so concentrated on their tasks that no one noticed us crossing the patio. Inside my room, Pedro kissed me tenderly. He took his time, sweetly.
He let our hands recognize each other, let the wall of ice that stood between us melt completely. We spent all morning making love, until Chencha called my name. The jewelry store had called on the telephone to ask why I hadn't picked up the

medallion. They had been expecting me. Before I left my room I tried to fix my hair and clothes as much as I could and tried to erase the satisfaction from my face. When I exited I realized I couldn't walk well because my legs were trembling. And with good reason. I'm practically still a virgin at 37 and I'm getting too old for these physical exertions.

Mother always said that duty comes first, before anything, especially pleasure. As a girl this mandate caused me a lot of headaches. I had no trouble understanding that things needed to follow a certain order. "Of course," thought my childish brain, "without flowers there can be no honey. Without chickens there can be no eggs. Without sheep there can be no wool." I only got confused when I had to categorize something as either duty or pleasure. It didn't take long for me to understand that duty meant everything mother ordered us to do and pleasure meant everything we liked and had to leave for later. Knowing her personal history, I now realize that mother, like myself, had to learn this the hard way. She had to set her personal desires aside to tend to a family she would have wanted to raise with someone else. I wonder if it wouldn't have been better for her to follow her heart instead of the obligations imposed by others.

Who can define duty anyhow?
For example, I thought that it was my duty to change the destiny of this family and I accomplished it, yet I'm still not sure about the long-term results of my actions. I wish I could have a crystal ball so I could see how Esperanza will raise her sons and daughters. She has received the best education from all those who love her. From Rosaura she learned to sew, embroider, play piano and sing. From Pedro she learned mathematics and administration. From John she learned biology and chemistry. Shirley taught her first aid and the use of medicinal plants to treat certain ailments. And I passed on to her the secrets of the kitchen, the results of shaping dough with one's hands. The influence of the stars on agriculture. The best time to water plants. How to ask permission from a plant before cutting a branch. The rituals that allow us to become one with nature so we can think like a tree, like a river, like wind,

like fire. How to honor, care and protect this natural world which we are a part of. That, I think, is our duty, and Esperanza understands it well. Now it will be her responsibility to transmit this knowledge to her children. I can't wait to see her become a mother. To see her children grow, see how she raises them, to take their photograph when they take their first steps, to celebrate their first words, to feed them their first bean soup, their first corn tortilla.

I don't know why we always look to the past instead of to the present. I look at the kitchen table and I am invaded by countless memories. This table has borne witness to so much sorrow, so much joy, countless celebrations. Here I have spent most of my 37 years of life. What is more, I was born on it. And now it's incredible to think that it's the last time I shall cook for Esperanza at this table. I may cook for her again, but only when she comes to visit. The family life we have built together is now a thing of the past. I awoke sick with nostalgia. The idea of never seeing something or someone again shakes me to my core. Tomorrow, I will not see the same ranch. Esperanza, one of its most important inhabitants, will be gone. I know that my sadness is a bit absurd. Esperanza isn't dying, she is only getting married. I will see her many more times. But I feel that absence is like death. When one can no longer see or hear a loved one, it's like they no longer exist, like they're vanishing. I suddenly got the urge to take a photograph of the ranch, to capture it today because tomorrow it will be different. I took three separate pictures which I later developed and assembled on cardboard to see the entire panorama of the ranch. I plan to give it to Esperanza. Her wedding puts an end to my secret commitment to her. I can now design my new life and I feel funny. I'm not used to thinking about life as something to be enjoyed. Pedro and I have made great strides in that respect but we still don't feel completely free of all commitments. We have talked about taking a vacation after the wedding. Pedro says I should forget about cooking for some time, and he's right, but it's hard for me because the kitchen has been my refuge, my trench, my constant fountain of knowledge, my way of giving love. In all these years, except for the time I spent with John, I haven't had the opportunity to think about myself. All of my time, effort and thoughts were focused first on caring for mother, then for Esperanza. The first out of duty, the second out of love. Obligations kept my mind hazy and bewildered. And suddenly, tomorrow, that will all come to an end. I am close to freedom and I feel confused. I imagine it's similar to when Gertrudis was told that the Revolution was over and that she had to return to her civilian lifestyle. Although this may not be a valid comparison because it must be much easier to put down a rifle than to hang up an apron. I feel like a pot that is tired of boiling so much water, that cries out to be removed from the fire, but at the same time longs to remain in contact with the heat because it knows that if it cools too suddenly, it will crack. In the meantime I decided to end my days as the cook of this ranch on a high note. I decided to make Chiles in Nogada sauce for the wedding feast. We have been peeling walnuts for the past week and my fingers are stained from the tint of their skin. I have just decided that the best way to remove the stains is with a hot bath. I will take one before bed. I might even put chocolate in the bath water so that it can penetrate every pore of my skin while I also drink it, because I do believe I deserve a good cup of hot chocolate!

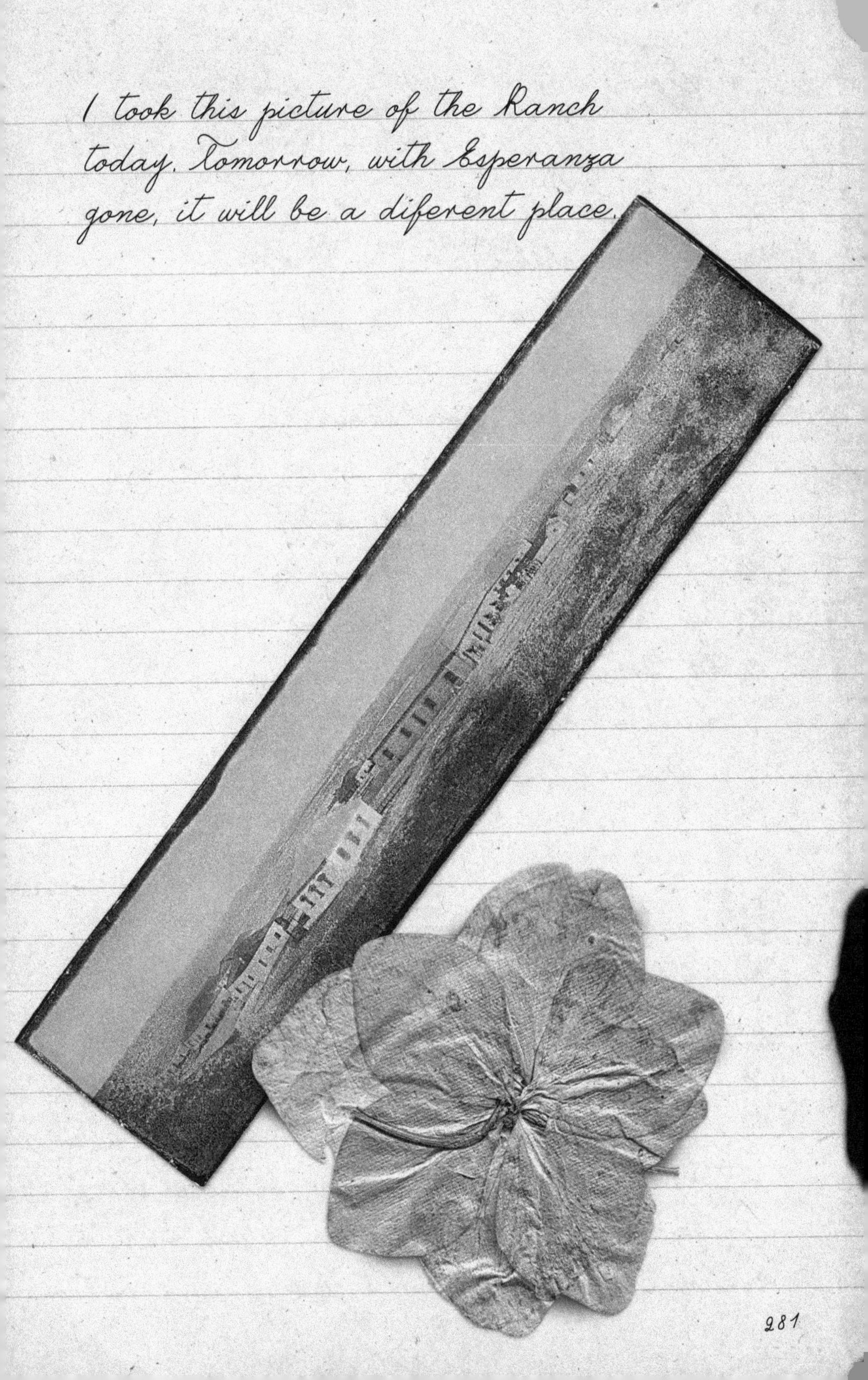

I took this picture of the Ranch today. Tomorrow, with Esperanza gone, it will be a diferent place.

Chiles in Nogada sauce

Ingredients:

25 poblano chiles
8 pomegranates
100 walnuts
100 grams aged queso fresco
1 kg ground beef
100 grams raisins
1/4 kg almonds
1/4 kg pecans
1/2 kg tomato
2 medium onions
2 candied citron
1 peach
1 apple
Cumin
White pepper
Salt
Sugar

Instructions:

The walnuts should be peeled days beforehand, because it is a very demanding job that takes many hours. After removing the shell of the walnuts, you must also remove the skin. Be very careful to not leave even a tiny piece of skin on them, because when the walnuts are ground and mixed with cream the skin will make this mixture bitter, invalidating all of your previous efforts. Once all walnuts are peeled, grind them in a metate along with the cheese and cream. Finally, add salt and white pepper to taste. This nogada sauce will be poured over the chiles and then garnished with the pomegranate.

Filling:

Fry the onion in a bit of oil. Once it is golden, add the ground beef, cumin and a bit of sugar. Once the meat is browned, add chopped peach, apple, nuts, raisins, almonds and tomato until its well seasoned. Then add salt to taste and let it dry before removing from the fire. Roast the poblano chiles and remove the skin. Then open on one side to remove veins and seeds, and stuff with filling.

Dear Diary,
I am writing a quick note before I leave for the church because I don't want to forget yesterday's experience. I could write about it tonight when all the guests have departed but I fear I will be so tired that I won't be able to even hold the pen.
Last night, I prepared a hot bath with some chocolate in it. As I relaxed my body in the water I sipped my ceremonial cup of hot chocolate. I made one for Pedro as well, but he drank it in his room.
I don't know if I put too much chocolate in mine, but as I drank not only did I feel an intense ecstasy, I also began to see lights. Little by little I was able to focus my vision and I saw Morning Light and Nacha lighting candles throughout my bedroom. As Nacha lit a candle she sat as I watched her, turned her head and said: "the light is now within you child, congratulations."
Suddenly I saw someone caressing my head and washing my hair just like I had

washed mother's hundreds of time in the same tub. I turned, and to my surprise and saw mother! She was dressed in white, a color she always avoided in life. She looked splendid, joyous and glowing, so much so that it was hard for me to recognize her. "Mother?" I asked, and she answered "yes dear child, it's me" as she dropped some orange blossoms into the tub. Her eyes were bright lights.

I heard her voice within me clearly say "You have accomplished your mission. Congratulations. Now rest. You turned out to be a better mother than I ever imagined. You gave Esperanza the freedom I was never able to give you. Fear overcame me and I surrendered to it. I had my power of decision taken from me, so I chose to control and dominate everyone, you in particular, without realizing that I was oppressing you the same way others oppressed me. I'm sorry I didn't allow you to marry. I didn't know what to do. I wish in life I could have had your courage, it certainly would have prevented me from making so many mistakes. But from where I am now, where everything is one, I live in you, I am fulfilled in you, I am forgiven in you, I love in you. From here I can say that I was wrong and I take back my words. If duty comes first, then love is our one and only duty and it must come before anything else. To love is both our duty and our pleasure. There is nothing before or after love, don't let it slip away from you Josefita." She then kissed my forehead as a farewell. I can't begin to explain the relief I felt in my heart. Well, now I must leave because I don't want to be late for the wedding.

Dear Tita:

I feel like an intruder, reading your intimate thoughts. I'm sorry, but your diary was the only thing we found under the charred remains of the ranch and I am clinging to it for dear life as it is the only thing I have left of you. Your departure has been my greatest loss. Now I understand why I always felt like you should have been my real mother. I never had the slightest clue about the great love between you and my father. I imagine that the two burnt and embraced bodies that were found in your room were you and him. That is what I want to believe. I took the liberty of writing in your diary because you had allowed me to before, as a child. You always made me feel like everything that was yours was mine as well, that it belonged to me. "Everything belongs to everyone" was your favorite phrase, and now I understand it. I will take your diary and your story of love as my inheritance. And I will try my best to honor such a grand, grand love. I will not let it go to waste. I will not let it die. May it come out into the light and shine upon us all.

Esperanza

Laura Esquivel

Started out as a teacher and a multi-awarded screenwriter. Her first novel, Like Water for Chocolate, has sold over seven million copies worldwide and has been translated to more than 30 languages. Other books written in her available in english are The Law of Love, Swift as Desire, Malinche, Pierced by the Sun, and The Colors of My Past, the last part of the Like Water for Chocolate Trilogy.

CPSIA information can be obtained
at www.ICGtesting.com
Printed in the USA
LVHW050501200122
708648LV00003B/106